SCREAMS IN SYMPHONY

KELSEY CLAYTON

Copyright © 2022 by Kelsey Clayton

All rights reserved.

No part of this book may be reproduced in any form or by any electronic or mechanical means, including information storage and retrieval systems, without written permission from the author, except for the use of brief quotations in a book review.

Editing by Kiezha Ferrell at Librum Artis
Cover by Y'all That Graphic

To Lisa.
So glad I have you.
Thank you for loving even the darkest parts of me.

P.S - You're still never allowed to move.

My love for you was bulletproof
    but you're the one who shot me.

— PIERCE THE VEIL

CHAPTER 1

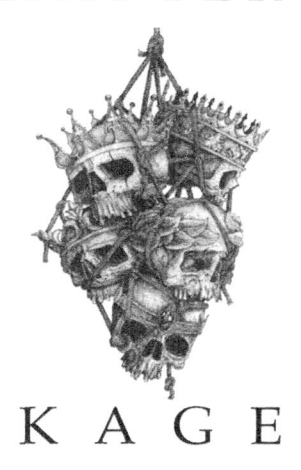

KAGE

R<small>AGE</small>.

It flows through my veins, charring everything in its path, the fire inside me being suffocated until it's nothing but glowing embers. Family and friends gather around to bid farewell to the one they love. The one ripped from us too soon. My fist clenches as I listen to those around me cry their fake tears, whispering about age-old memories they wouldn't have remembered if not for the current circumstance. And when they lower the casket into the ground, the last honorable part of me goes along with it.

Nothing but malice remains.
And mark my words.
I'm going to find him.
And I'm going to skin him alive.

Present Day

Firetrucks and an ambulance fill the street as we pull up. Onlookers stand across the street and watch the destruction unfold before their eyes. Flames rip through the house, destroying everything they touch and leaving behind nothing but soot and ash in its place. And the only thing I can think of is Saxon walking up those front porch steps not even fifteen minutes ago.

A window on the top floor shatters. Pieces of glass rain down as the fire bursts through the opening. I jump out of the car and take in the scene before me.

Firefighters dousing the leaping flames.

EMTs waiting dutifully at the ambulance.

A single police officer standing across the street to make sure people stay a safe distance away.

What I don't see, however, is any sight of Saxon.

I spare a glance at Nico only to find him staring in shock at the house he shared with his sister. Beni runs around the front of the car and the two of us share a look that silently says what we're both thinking.

If there's any chance of saving Saxon, we have to do it ourselves.

He follows behind me as I run toward the house, only to be stopped by a firefighter with a complex. He's doing nothing useful for anyone, just standing there barking orders while his men bust their asses doing the real work.

"Are you looking to get yourself killed?" he asks me. "Leave the heroics to the professionals."

I try to pass him, but he pushes me back with a hand on my chest. Smacking it away at his wrist, I glare at him.

"My girl is in there!"

He gives me a sorrowful look. "Sir, while I feel deeply for you, no one is allowed to enter that house. Neighbors reported gunshots before the fire started, and we don't know if the shooter is still inside."

A darkness settles over me as I grin and Beni slots himself between me and *Mr. Hero Complex*. "Oh, I hope like hell they are."

With Beni blocking him, I ignore the calls of protest behind me and run into the burning house. The smoke makes it impossible to see—or breathe. I quickly pull my shirt up over my mouth in an attempt to filter the air a little better.

"Saxon!" I shout, but I hear nothing except the crackling of the wood. "Sax!"

Beads of sweat start to form across my forehead from the overwhelming heat. I wipe it away with my sleeve and try calling out for her again, only to be met with the same response. *Nothing.*

"Get the fuck out of there!" someone bellows from outside.

But I can't.

I *won't*.

Not without Saxon.

The sound of something crashing beside me has me dropping down to shield for cover, but as I do, my foot slips out from under me and my hands catch my fall. They feel wet. Coated in a familiar substance. And my heart sinks when I immediately know what it is.

No.

I drop down further only to find a puddle of blood, and in the middle of it is Saxon. She's unconscious. Her pale skin is waxy, devoid of the life it held only hours ago when I last saw her, and the amount of blood on the floor sends a shot of pain through my chest I haven't felt in decades.

It's brutal.

Excruciating.

Overwhelming.

Picking Saxon up in my arms, I hold her close to my chest and carry her outside. I try not to pay attention to how light she feels, or how lifeless, but it's there in the background— screaming at my subconscious.

Two EMTs rush over from the ambulance while the third opens the back of the ambulance and grabs the stretcher. As one reaches to take her from me, I give him a look that dares him to touch her.

"I've got her," I growl.

They follow me over to the ambulance as I lay her down on the stretcher. Immediately, they get to work on her. All of the blood makes it hard to locate where it's coming from, but they move quickly.

"Pulse is weak," the one barks.

The second lifts her shirt just slightly to check her stomach, and that's when he sees it. "Two bullet holes in the lower abdomen. We're losing her. We have to get her to the hospital, and fast."

As they work together loading the stretcher into the ambulance, I look down at my suit to find I'm covered in blood. And even worse, I'm covered in *her* blood. And just like that, I'm ten years old again and reliving one of the worst days of my life.

"Sir, are you coming?"

I snap my attention back where it's needed and climb into the ambulance. I turn to Beni, who stares anxiously at Saxon's motionless body.

"Meet us at the hospital," I demand.

He nods, and just as the EMT closes the doors, my eyes meet Nico's.

I'll deal with him later.

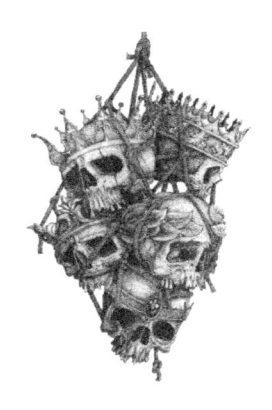

THE WAITING ROOM IS a grim place, filled with many different people all feeling the same emotion. *Fear.* There aren't a lot of things that scare me in the world. And after everything I've been through, no one could blame me for that. But losing the one woman who can silence my demons with just the sound of her name? That scares the fucking shit out of me.

Beni comes in to find me pacing the room, running my fingers through my hair without realizing that they're still stained red from her blood. He rushes over to me, and I can already tell he's feeling the same thing I am right now, only less intensely.

"What's going on?" he questions. "Is she going to be okay?"

I shake my head. "I don't know. She's in surgery."

Chaos and danger are things I have always handled well, but not today. Today my stomach churns with the unknown and my body feels like it could give out at any given moment. I'm running on nothing but straight adrenaline and crippling anxiety.

"Shit," he murmurs, mainly to himself. "Have they given you any information at all?"

"No. She flatlined twice in the ambulance, and when we

got here, they rushed her straight into surgery," I explain. "I was told to wait here, but how the fuck am I just supposed to sit here and wait?"

He pulls his phone out of his pocket and brings it to his ear. "Bring a change of clothes for Kage to Langone Hospital. Call me when you get here."

As he hangs up the phone, he looks at me and exhales. "She's strong as hell. She's going to pull through this."

And I want to believe him, but after watching her die twice, I'm afraid to hope.

I MANAGE TO FIND a way to distract myself. Now, is it healthy that I'm thinking of everything humanly possible to find Viola? Probably not. And are the things I'm imagining doing to her going to get me a ticket into heaven? Definitely not, but it's also not like my fate wasn't already sealed. One more brutalized body is not going to tip the scales.

The new clothes Beni had Cesari bring me are easier to sit in than the blood-soaked ones that were left in a clear bag, looking like something straight out of a horror movie. And if I wasn't determined not to leave this area until I get an update on Saxon, I would have followed Ces out just to see the weird looks he was given on his way to the car.

I swipe at my phone, opening emails that I'm only half reading because I don't have the mindset to pay attention to anything other than the outcome of this surgery. But when I see one from Mattia, it clicks.

My fingers move across my phone rapidly as I type out an email, telling him I want the location of Viola Mancini as soon as he can possibly get it, when Beni bumps my arm. I quickly look his way, only to see him looking at someone else.

The moment my eyes land on Nico, I see nothing but red. It takes all of three seconds before I'm out of my chair, with my hand wrapped tightly around Nico's throat while I pin him to the wall.

"What the fuck did you and your psycho of a sister do?" I roar.

He grasps at my wrist, trying to pull my hand away with no luck. "Nothing, I swear."

His breathing is cut off, but not enough to pass out just yet as I get closer into his face. "Bullshit. You expect me to believe that she went to meet your other half and wound up with two shots in the gut, and you had *nothing* to do with it?"

"Kage," he croaks out. "Please."

As his face starts to turn purple, I release him and he falls to the ground, coughing and gasping for air. I stand over him, looking down at the scum he is and wondering why I let anything stop me from killing him before. There's no part of this piece of shit—or the bitch he shared a womb with—that deserves to live, and once he gives me what I need, I'm going to rectify that.

There will be no more getting away with undermining my authority, his father's feelings be damned.

"You have a lot of balls showing up here," I sneer. "Or did you think they'd have a better chance of saving your life if I kill you *at* the hospital?"

He looks up at me with fear and panic in his eyes. "Boss, I swear on everything, I had nothing to do with this."

The name catches me off guard, but it earns him no points. He gets no respect from me. "If that's true, you'll find Viola and deliver her to me."

"Why? So you can kill her?"

I rear back and send a hard kick into his ribcage, thankful that Beni is blocking everyone's view. He curls into a ball, and I bend down. Gripping his collar, I pull him up until he's forced to face me.

"You do not ask questions," I tell him. "If you want to live, you will find the little cunt and bring her to me. Otherwise, I'll track her down myself and kill you both. The choice is yours."

He says nothing as I pull him to his feet and pretend for our audience's sake that he just fell. It isn't until he goes to walk away that he stops and turns back to me.

"She's family."

I scoff. "The *Familia* doesn't turn against its own. You have three days."

Chapter 2

Saxon

ALL THE PAIN SUBSIDES AS I FIND MYSELF IN A PEACEFUL MEADOW. *I feel as if I'm nothing, but at the same time everything. Like I'm here, there, everywhere. As if I've left the restraints of Earth and can move freely. Brightly colored flowers fill the area, and the grass is a shade of green that reminds me of spring. The sun shines brightly, warming my skin and restoring a sense of calmness.*

A familiar face in the distance tugs at my heartstrings.

Grandpa.

He's sitting on a bench, looking exactly the way I like to remember him, with his jeans and a button-down shirt he leaves open to show the T-shirt underneath. His hair is back to the thick brown it was when I was younger, pushed back and away from his face in a James Dean style.

Upon getting closer, I notice he's holding something. A baby, wrapped in a blue blanket. He smiles down at him, rocking him slowly and playing with him the same way he used to with Kylie and me. There's something about him I can't put my finger on, but it's wiped from my mind the second my grandfather's gaze meets mine.

"Saxon," he breathes.

He puts the baby down into a bed of flowers and stands, wrapping his arms around me. The smell of his cologne brings me back to Christmas mornings on his lap, with cookies and hot chocolate.

"You shouldn't be here."

I look around. "I'm not sure I know where here *is."*

Instead of answering me, he sighs. "Let's take a walk, shall we?"

Nodding, I take his hand, and we head on our way. I take everything in. How the sky is so blue, and it feels like nothing can go wrong. It's intoxicatingly peaceful. But the second I blink, we're somewhere else. Somewhere horribly familiar.

Fire rips through a house despite all the effort firefighters are putting in to stop it. I watch with wide eyes until it comes back to me. Walking up those porch stairs. Stepping inside and not being able to see in the darkness.

I gasp.

"She shot me." A tear slips out and slides down my cheek. "Why would she do that to me?"

He gives me a sad smile. "Oh, Wildflower. Love is such a strong and demanding emotion. Some people can't help but to let it cloud their judgment."

I close my eyes, and my mind goes to Kage. The way I feel about him is unlike anything I've ever known. It's as if my lungs don't know how to breathe unless we're taking in the same air. It's toxic, and dependent, and unhealthy, but God—it's everything.

"Yeah," my grandfather says. "You know it well."

My eyes open, and we're standing in the middle of what looks to be a hospital waiting room. Kage is sitting next to Beni, his leg bouncing impatiently. It looks like he's aged seven years in the course of a couple hours. The lines in his forehead are going to be set into place from being so tense.

"He's worried about me."

"As he should be."

I glance back at my grandfather. "And yet you still don't approve of me being with him."

Shaking his head, he grins softly and comes closer. "It's not him I don't approve of. Kage is a good man, despite what he believes about himself. It's just the lifestyle I don't want for you."

"It was good enough for you," I counter.

"I lived in a different time, Wildflower."

My attention goes back to Kage, and I try to run my fingers through his hair, but he doesn't feel it. I want to get him to see me. To tell him that I'm okay and to stop worrying, but I can't. I'm not really here.

"We have to go," my grandfather tells me, taking my hand once more.

He pulls me away and leads me down a hallway and into an operating room. At first, I'm not sure why we're here, but then I see it. It's me. I'm lying on a table while doctors work intensively to save my life.

"Oh my God," I croak.

Going closer, I see why Kage is so worried, and why my grandfather said that he should be. To say I'm in bad shape would be an understatement. One of the doctors orders for more blood while the other has his hands inside my stomach.

"Am I going to die?"

Grandpa hums. "That one is up to you, my dear."

"I found the other one," the doctor says. "Forceps."

I watch with increasing dread as he pulls a bullet from my stomach, and at that moment, I know. My chest tightens. No. I run my hand over my hand over my own cheek, as if it's not my own body I'm looking at.

She's fighting for her life, with no idea what kind of life she's fighting for.

"And what if I don't want to go back?"

My grandfather's voice sounds from behind me. "Then you'll stay here with us."

I turn around to find him holding the same baby from earlier, and I know it in my heart.

This is my baby.

Grandpa puts him in my arms, and as he grips my finger, I'm back *in the meadow. Two big, brown eyes blink up at me, and happiness radiates from him as he smiles. He looks so much like Kage, just with my dimples. I hold him tighter, resting my forehead against his and breathing him in.*

I don't know if I can leave this place without him.

CHAPTER 3

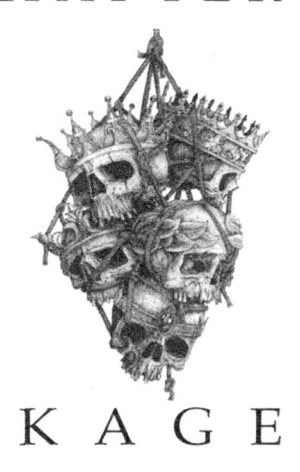

KAGE

PATIENCE IS NOT MY STRONG SUIT. BY THE THIRD hour, I've run out of things to distract myself with. And by the fourth, every person to come through the door has me on edge. With the amount of pacing I've done today, Beni says I should be wearing one of those watches that tracks your steps. I'd be hitting new records.

My phone vibrates in my pocket, and I pull it out to see Raff calling for the third time. Just like the two times before, I hit ignore and put it back in my pocket. It's not that this was *his* doing, and I'm sure he's genuinely worried about Saxon's wellbeing, but the last thing I want to hear right now is about how Viola is family and we should hear her out first.

I have no intentions of doing that, no matter what he has to say.

She will pay for the damage she has caused with her life, and I cannot wait to watch her fucking suffer.

IT'S THE MIDDLE OF hour number six when Beni sighs after receiving a text message. He dials a number and puts the phone to his ear. I can't hear the other end of the call, but judging by my underboss's grim tone, it can't be good.

"Call Dante down at the morgue. Make sure it's Dante and Dante *only* that comes to get him. We don't know any of the new guys they have over there, and they haven't been vetted yet," he says. "And Ro? Thanks for handling things."

He hangs up the phone and drops it into his lap, looking over at me. Keeping his voice low, even though there's only one elderly couple in the room with us, he fills me in on what happened.

"It's Paolo. Roman found him in the bushes by the front door, throat slit from ear to ear."

I grunt. "Well, that explains how Saxon was able to leave so easily."

My blood boils. Not only did Viola attempt to kill Saxon, but she took out one of my men. I always knew she was psychotic, but I never thought she would stoop this low. As much as I respect Raff, he failed at teaching them the meaning of family he preaches so much about.

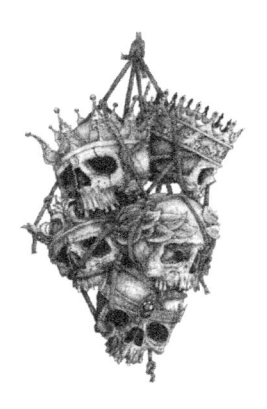

I'VE COME TO THE conclusion that nothing can put me at ease. There have been plenty of moments in my life where my patience has been tested, hence how I know I don't possess any, but this is worse than I could ever imagine. The wait is excruciating, and the only thing to bring comfort is knowing that if she were dead, they would have come to tell me that by now.

Seconds after that thought passes through my mind, the door opens, and I silently curse myself for potentially manifesting the worst thing to happen to me in my adult years. Hell, losing her might be the worst thing to happen to me in my entire life.

I mentally prepare myself for the lines everyone knows but no one wants to hear.

We did all we could.

The damage was too extensive.

Despite our efforts, we were unable to save her.

"Saxon Forbes?" he calls out. I stand from my chair and he comes my way. "Are you family?"

"I'm her husband," I answer without missing a beat.

Beni chuckles quietly beside me, but plays it off as something on his phone. I pay him no attention, too busy focusing everything I have on not losing it on this doctor. He's taking way too long to tell me how Saxon is, and if he doesn't start talking soon, there's no saying what I'll do.

"Your wife suffered two gunshot wounds to the stomach. Due to her injuries, she lost a lot of blood," he explains. "We had to replace nearly half of her blood supply during surgery, and because of that, while we were able to get the bleeding under control, it's going to be a waiting game to see when and *if* she wakes up."

A drop of relief runs through me because she isn't dead yet, but the doctor's news is anything but good. I exhale and drop my head, nodding as I take it all in, when he speaks again.

"And unfortunately, due to the location of the injuries, we were unable to save the baby."

Both mine and Beni's heads snap up at that, and my mouth runs dry. "Baby? What baby?"

His brows furrow. "Your wife was in the earlier stages of a pregnancy." In the worst possible timing, his pager goes off and he looks down at it. "I'm so sorry. Another patient of mine needs my attention, but they will come get you when your wife is settled in the ICU."

He walks away, completely unaware of the mental turmoil he just created. I sit down slowly, feeling Beni's eyes on me the whole time. There are a million things running through my mind, not the least of which is being eighteen years old and freshly healed from a vasectomy when a doctor came in and told me that it was successful and there was no trace of sperm in my semen.

"I want you to scour through all of the interior footage we have over the last month," I order Beni. "If she was fucking someone else, I want to know who."

He takes a deep breath and turns to his phone. "Boss, respectfully, that doesn't sound like Saxon to me. And besides, if you do the math, the timeline adds up."

He may be right. It doesn't sound like Saxon. And the last few weeks we've spent tangled together, not knowing where one ends and the other begins. But the fact of the matter is she *didn't* tell me, and that's enough to make me question everything.

"Fucking humor me."

"Yes, sir."

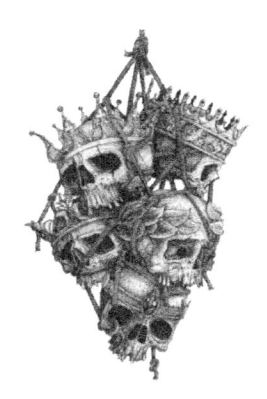

ANOTHER WHOLE HOUR PASSES before someone comes to show me where Saxon is. I follow the nurse down the corridor and into the elevator. A tense silence settles between us, like she knows better than to ask how my day is going. When it finally opens, she leads me through double doors and into the ICU.

The wheezing sound of ventilators come from almost every room we pass. Glass doors allow the nurses to watch all the patients' monitors from outside the room, and crying family members are a dime a dozen. There are a million different places I've pictured Saxon, most of them naked, but here is definitely not one of them.

As we turn the corner, the nurse stops outside of a room and gives me a warm smile before gesturing for me to enter. Every step I take feels heavy. Walking into her room feels like hell, and despite all the chaos and pain I've experienced in my thirty-four years, nothing could prepare me for seeing her like this.

At first glance, she looks peaceful, but as I walk around the bed, I realize how untrue that is. Her skin is pale, lacking the pink tint to her cheeks I'm so accustomed to. There are still remnants of soot from the fire in her hair, and I can only imagine what's hidden beneath the gown she has on. The only thing assuring me that she's alive is the beeping of the machine and the rise and fall of her chest as she breathes.

I bend down and press a kiss to her forehead. She looks so fragile. Like if I add too much pressure, she'll shatter. So, I keep my touch light.

"You have to be okay," I whisper into her ear. "I need you to be okay."

I SPEND MORE TIME than I'd like to admit wondering where we went wrong. Where *I* went wrong. The fact that she didn't tell me about the baby cuts deeper than I thought it would. And hoping that she didn't know herself is both selfish and selfless, because I don't know how or *if* she can recover from that.

A knock at the door has me looking away from Saxon to

find Dr. Ferro at the door. He's dressed in his white coat, which must mean he's working here today. Seeing him here brings a new sense of relief, because after all, he isn't our personal doctor for his smile.

"Antonio," I stand to greet him. "I'm so glad you're here. While I'm sure the competence of your colleagues is up to par, I trust your expertise immensely."

He tilts his head to the side. "I wasn't called here to check on Saxon. Beni told me to come get a sample from you. He said you're concerned about the current status of your vasectomy."

Fucking Beni. "The doctor said that Saxon was pregnant at the time of the shooting. She lost the baby, but I'm supposed to be sterile. Seriously though, I can worry about this later. She's my concern right now."

He nods. "How about this; you take this cup and go get me a sample, and while I wait, I'll look over Saxon and her chart to put your mind at ease."

My phone vibrates, and I pull it out to see a text from the devil himself.

Beni: Better to know than to let it drive you insane.

Much to my dismay, Beni and the doc both have a point, so I reluctantly take the supplies and head into the bathroom. It isn't until I step inside, however, that I realize the chances of me getting hard right now, let alone being able to finish, are gravely slim.

Still, I open the cup and place it on the counter before unzipping my pants. My cock is soft as I wrap my hand around it, and for the first few minutes, there isn't anything I can do to change that. It isn't until I close my eyes and let images of Saxon run through my mind that it starts to stir.

I can feel the blood flow south, and I harden in my hand as I picture her on her knees in front of me, her mouth wide open, begging for me to fill it. After the first time she sucked my dick, she made it a point to get better at it. And goddamn, did she ever. When she puts her mind to it, I don't think there's anything that woman *can't* do.

I stroke myself faster, feeling my muscles clench as I get closer—imagining my hand is her mouth, taking me all the way in until she fucking chokes on it. And by the time I'm close, I'm damn near strangling my cock.

"Come on, badass," she teases. *"Fill my mouth with your cum. I want the taste of you on my tongue for the rest of the day."*

All the anger and frustration I've bottled up all day is being taken out on myself. My pace quickens as my fist gets tighter, and by the time I'm about to come, I'm scrambling for the cup and emptying everything I have into it.

For a single moment, I feel better. All the stress of the day is gone, but when I look at the cup and realize what it could mean, it all comes rushing back. Knowing I could bear a child brings its own share of questions and decisions, but possibly finding out that Saxon was sleeping with someone else? That would bring blood and violence that no one has ever seen before.

I slip the cup into the paper bag and wash my hands. When I'm done, I walk out to find Antonio reading Saxon's chart. He flips it closed and hands it back to the nurse, thanking her softly.

"All done?" he questions.

I nod and hand him the bag. "Anything I should be concerned about?"

Antonio has one hell of a poker face. It's practically required in his line of work. But after working with him for years, I know every one of his tells, and this one isn't good.

"The damage was extensive," he admits. "While the bullet missed her major organs, it wreaked havoc on her insides. If you hadn't gotten to her when you did, she would have bled out only moments later. The doctor was right when he said it's a waiting game at this point."

"So, all I can do is pray for the best?"

He looks over at Saxon and smiles. "I've treated many people in my time, but not many are as strong and as stubborn as she is. Don't give up hope just yet. And yes, a little prayer is never a bad idea."

With a pat on my shoulder, he tells me he will have the results for me in a couple of hours. And then he leaves me alone to imagine a million different possibilities.

What a life with Saxon would be like.

What a *family* with Saxon would be like.

And the unavoidable, what a life *without* Saxon would be like.

That one I don't think I could bear at all.

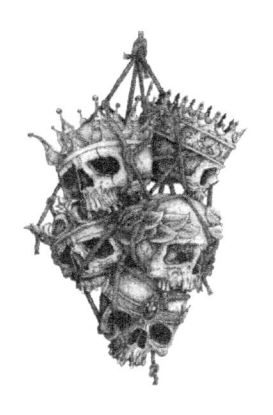

THERE'S SOMETHING PEACEFUL IN watching someone's breathing. The steady rise and fall of their chest. The sound of it reminding you that they're alive and putting your fears at ease. I never really understood why some people like to watch others sleep until now. Because sitting here, watching her, I could do this for hours and never tire of it.

She's stronger than this. Hell, she damn near killed

herself because she wouldn't let *me* win. To believe for a second she would let Viola take her out is an insult to the whole institution that is Saxon Royce Forbes.

My gaze moves down to her stomach, and for the first time, I allow myself to feel the loss of what could have been. I wonder what he or she would have looked like. Would they have their mother's eyes? My temper? For the love of God, give them anything but my temper. Then again, I've seen Saxon's, and that may not be much better.

The sound of her stirring has my heart damn near leaping out of my chest. Immediately, I'm on my feet and at her bedside. My hand grips hers, and I speak softly to her.

"Saxon? Baby, are you there?"

Her eyes flutter open, and as she looks at me, the corners of her mouth twitch into what's almost a smile, until it takes a turn for the worst.

I watch her eyes roll into the back of her head, and my stomach sinks deeper than when I heard the shots through the phone. Monitors start to go crazy, and within seconds, her room is flooded with nurses and doctors. I'm pushed out of the way by a nurse who doesn't have the time to ask me to move.

"What's wrong with her?" I ask.

But no one hears me. They talk among themselves, using medical terms that I wish I had Antonio here to translate. It isn't until they're unhooking things and rushing her out of the room that a nurse stops to look at me.

She hangs back for a second as they push Saxon down the hall. "Your wife is having complications. We need to get her back into surgery and fast."

I nod, mumbling a quiet thank you while feeling like every part of me is dying inside. As she dashes off to join everyone else, I'm left in an empty room. Wires that were attached to Saxon only moments ago hang from the machines, and I'm faced with the brutal reality of what could very well be my life.

A life without her.

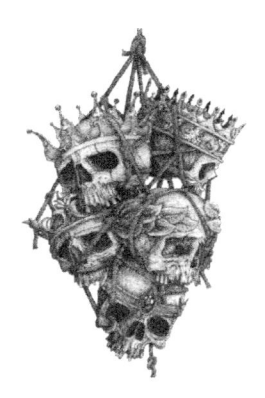

BENI COMES INTO THE room, only to be faced with me sitting in a chair—a plastic cup of whiskey gripped firmly in my hand. He glances around, as if Saxon is going to pop out from behind a curtain. When he notices the empty spot where her bed should be, his brows furrow.

"What's going on? Where is she?"

I chuckle humorlessly. "One of the nurses said I look like I need a drink." I hold up the cup. "I'm not sure whether to be impressed that she carries whiskey in her purse, or concerned that she's drinking on the job."

He takes a few steps toward me, cautiously. As if I'm a rabid animal. "Kage. Where is Saxon?"

I stare back at him, feeling the lump in my throat that prevents me from answering the question. I stand up and start to head out of the room, but stop when I'm right beside him.

"You were right, you know," I confess. "Doc said that my vasectomy reversed itself. The baby she was pregnant with? It was mine."

Neither of us say anything else as I walk by him and out into the hall.

I lost my baby.
A baby I didn't even know existed.
And chances are, I'm going to lose her, too.

CHAPTER 4

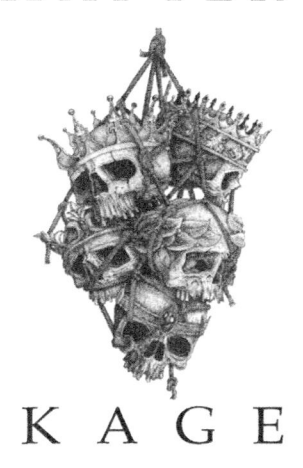

KAGE

Pain is a dangerous thing. It can make people crazy. Turn them into something they swore they would never become. And once you give into the pain, there's no guarantee you'll ever come back from it.

I stand in front of my mirror, fixing my suit and adjusting my tie. A welcome numbness settles over me. I've spent enough time feeling an overwhelming load of emotions.

Anger.

Sadness.

Fear.

Devastation.

But today, there will be no emotion from me, because my enemies—the men who want nothing more than to see me fall—they feed off of weakness, and I refuse to show them any. They won't get that power from me.

There's a light knock on my door before it opens and Raff appears. He's dressed to the nines, with his Rolex shining against his wrist. His gray facial hair is properly groomed, and his hair is professionally styled.

"Son," he greets me.

"Raff."

I haven't seen or spoken to him recently, except for telling him what time to be here. Other than that, all communication has gone through Beni. It's not that I hold anything directly against Raff. It's not entirely his fault that his children put themselves at the top spot of my hit list. Honestly, I haven't spoken to anyone.

There hasn't been anything to say.

But being as he's here, it wouldn't be me if I didn't try to take advantage of the situation.

"Had any interesting encounters lately?" I ask. "Maybe had a visit from two spoiled brats desperate for Daddy's help?"

He exhales. "I don't know where they are, Kage, but even if I did, you can't honestly expect me to tell you. They're my kids."

"And according to you, so am I."

"You are," he argues back. "But I wouldn't just stand by as Nico kills *you*. We're family."

I scoff. "Exactly. Family. *La Familia.* And for someone who preaches about having loyalty to it, you seem to have none. Don't try to play like you don't know what she did."

"I know nothing because I haven't spoken to her. But if she did in fact do this, it was on someone else's orders, I can promise you that. Viola wouldn't do this on her own."

"You're partially right," I tell him. "It wasn't entirely her doing. We believe others, like Saxon's father, played a part, but trust me—she was a very willing participant."

He stays firm. "I have a hard time believing that."

Having heard enough, I pull my phone from my pocket and swipe to the video Beni sent me a week ago. It's from the night Saxon barged into my office and shocked the hell out of me by taking charge of a meeting with four made men.

After Raff had spoken to her outside, she came back

inside and kissed me before excusing herself for a moment. At the time, I thought she just needed to get her emotions under control. Finding out yet another person you trusted all but turned their back on you isn't easy. However, while searching through everything like I told Beni to do, he came across footage from one of the bathrooms that night.

"Saxon was pregnant with my child," I tell Raff as he watches the video. "Your prized moron found out and told his homicidal counterpart. My guess is she couldn't handle someone else bearing my child, since she's been obsessed with me since we were sixteen."

His eyes widen as he brings his attention back to me. "She's your sister."

I click my tongue against the roof of my mouth. "Yeah, it seems you're the only one who looks at it that way."

Taking my phone back, I slip it into my pocket. Raff goes silent and crosses his arms over his chest, clearly trying to work it all out in his head. I may not have convinced him of her guilt, but I at least poked holes into whatever excuse he's cooked up in his head to justify her actions.

"Now let's go," I tell him. "We have a funeral to attend, and we need to show a united front."

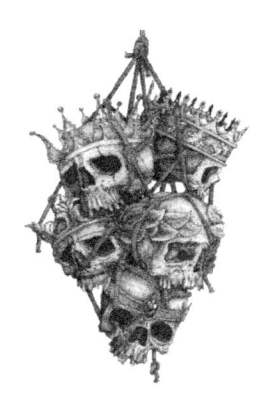

GRAY CLOUDS FILL THE sky. The dreary weather matches my mood, along with everyone else's. A large display of flowers sit on an easel, wrapping around an enlarged picture of the beauty that was Saxon Forbes. In it, she's wearing a sparkling gold dress. Her hair hangs off one shoulder, and she's sporting a wide grin, the infectious kind that could put anyone in a good mood just by being around her.

Her younger sister, Kylie, stands with her family, crying quietly as she stares at the casket. The heartbreak she's feeling is written all over her face. Dalton stands behind her, with his hands resting gently on her shoulders. Not exactly comforting her, but letting her know he's there.

I can't help but wonder what he has in the plans for her, because Dalton is a planner to a fault. He probably already has her fate written in a sealed envelope and waiting until she's eighteen to be opened. After all, I saw firsthand what he did to Saxon when she failed to follow his master plan.

Scarlett and Nessa are standing beside him, finding comfort in each other. Unrelenting tears flow down each of their faces as they grip each other tightly. The pain radiating off of them shows how loved Saxon truly was.

Well, at least by everyone but her father. He looks upset, but I know it's only for appearance's sake. After all, he knows exactly who is responsible for this and the part he played in it.

As I enter the conference room, Forbes is already there. He stands up, sporting a cocky little grin that makes it clear he thinks he's winning here, and takes a step toward me.

"Mr. Malvagio," he greets me, putting his hand out for me to shake.

I stare down at it and then look back at him. This is the man who wanted to give Saxon away to one of the men who killed my father, for nothing more than personal gain. That alone makes it so he doesn't deserve a single ounce of my respect. And everything else he's done just seals his fate.

"I have to say, I'm glad we're coming to an agreement," he says as he pulls his hand back and we sit down across from each other. "As you can imagine, I'm desperate to get my daughter back, and I'm sure you need to regain control of the city."

It takes everything in me not to roll my eyes, but it's important not to show any emotions. My face stays firm, not giving anything away. Mauricio takes the seat beside me and pulls the paperwork out of his briefcase. When he's done, all attention turns back to me.

"Let's get this over with."

The smile drops right off his face and he nods. "Of course."

Leaning forward, I lay my arms on the table. "It's come to my attention that you have ended up on the wrong side of Dmitri Petrov."

He grunts, but keeps his composure. "Yes, well, I guess I have you to thank for that."

I can't help but smile as I stick my tongue in my cheek. "Oh, I promise you, it was my pleasure."

His fist clenches on the table, but he knows better than to retaliate. Even looking at me the wrong way would result in him leaving here in a body bag, and while Dalton may not care about the life of anyone else, Saxon was right when she said he values his own.

"Enough small talk," I tell him. "I'm willing to offer you protection from the Bratva, and in return, you sign over the rights to everything you stole from me."

His brows raise. "That's it? You want me to hand over half of Manhattan in exchange for keeping me safe against something that may or may not happen?"

I shrug and go to stand. "I mean, if you think you don't need it, suit yourself."

"Fine!" he snaps. "Let's not be too hasty."

Sitting back down, I watch him expectantly and wait for him to continue.

"The Bratva was willing to offer me more, a lot more, in exchange for my inheritance."

"And to my understanding, that deal fell through," I counter. "Why does that matter to me?"

He smirks. "Because there are plenty of other crime organizations I'm sure would be interested in some of the properties I've acquired."

The longer I sit in front of this man, the more he manages to piss me off. "If you expect me to offer you power, you're going to be disappointed."

"And why's that?"

I square my shoulders. "Because the Familia is all about trust and loyalty, and lately all you've shown us is that you have none."

He throws his head back, laughing like there's humor to be found in this. "Oh, come on. You would've done the same if given the chance."

"Don't act like you and I are alike. I would never be as idiotic as to piss off not one crime family, but two. No amount of power is worth having that size of a target on your back."

"Coming from the man who has all of it," he counters. "Come on. I'm not looking for anything top level. Make me a Capo de Capi. You're lacking in one of those for this area."

It makes me uncomfortable to know that he's still aware of some of the inner workings of our organization. Andrea, my Capo for the city, was gunned down almost a year ago. We retaliated immediately, and the Bratva lost five of their men in exchange for my one. Since then, Raff has been trying to get me to promote Nico. It's his hope that he and I can get along and work together in a greater capacity, but that will happen over my dead body.

"I'll tell you what I'll do," I say. "Against my better judgment, I will allow you back into the family, but you're starting from the bottom."

"An associate? You may as well spit in my face."

"A soldati," I correct him. "No grunt work, but you have to work your way up like everyone else."

He glares at me. "I wanted power."

"And you're getting it. Being in the organization *is* power."

Leaning back in his chair, he taps his fingers against the table like he's considering it. Like there's actually something to consider. I already didn't want to come here, but to watch him act as if I'm not offering him a lifeline right now against my better judgment? Well, that makes me want to wrap my hands around his throat even more.

"I don't have all night, Forbes," I say sternly. "And I'm not a man whose time you want to waste. Sign the papers before I take back my offer."

Dalton picks up a pen and grabs one of the papers Mauricio passes to him, but just before he signs, he stops. "How do I know my daughter is still alive?"

I can feel as the little patience I have gets chipped away some more. "I can show you the scratch marks she left on my back last night. How's that sound?"

Nico coughs to disguise a laugh while Beni fights off a smile beside me. If this motherfucker wants to play games, we can play.

His grip on the paper tightens, crumpling it in the middle. "Fuck you, you piece of shit."

"No. Fuck *you*. Don't sit here and pretend like you give a shit about her."

It's as if something clicks and changes inside Dalton as he drops the act and smiles menacingly. "You're right. I don't. At least not after she became useless to Dmitri by sleeping with the likes of you." A dark laugh emits from the back of his throat. "But I happen to know that you do, which is why I can't wait to watch this destroy you."

My eyes narrow as Beni leans over. "He's stalling."

Dalton overhears and chuckles. "Am I? Or am I simply the decoy?"

A pit settles in my stomach as I look over at Roman. "Call Paolo and make sure Saxon is safe."

He nods and disappears into the back of the room, while Dalton sits there with a smug grin. A grin I'd like nothing more than to wipe right off of his face. The room goes silent, aside from Dalton's whistling, until Ro comes back.

"He didn't answer," he tells me.

Dalton hums. "I figured that would be the case. Poor guy. I hope he's okay."

Within seconds I'm out of my seat and across the table. I grab Dalton by the collar and pin him to the wall. "Tell me what the fuck you've done before I rip your head straight off your neck."

"You were right about loyalty," he sneers. "It's a valuable asset, when they're truly loyal to you."

I pull out my knife and press it to his throat, feeling the give as it presses into his skin.

"Go ahead," he taunts. "Kill me. It won't matter. By the time you get to Saxon, she'll already be dead."

The night I took Saxon's virginity, I honestly thought I was saving her. Sure, wanting her more than the air I breathe played a part in me giving into the idea so easily, but knowing that I was making her useless to Dmitri was my main intention. I had no idea that Dalton would stoop as low as playing a part in his own daughter's murder.

I underestimated my enemy, and that won't ever happen again.

As they lower the casket into the ground, Nessa finally reaches her breaking point. She lets out a pained noise and falls to the ground. Scarlett drops with her, rubbing her arm and holding her close. Everyone around watches helplessly as the girl who lost her best friend lies in the grass and weeps.

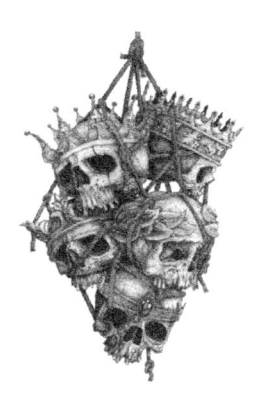

THE FUNERAL ENDS WITH the casket in its rightful place and covered with flowers. People pay their respects to her family and leave, sniffling as they wipe their eyes with tissues. Raff takes the lead as we step up to her family. He addresses Scarlett directly, being as he's closest with her.

"We are so sorry for your loss," he says kindly, taking her hand. "Saxon was an extraordinary young woman. Silas always talked about her like she was his pride and joy."

A sob rips through Scarlett, but she holds it together. "Thank you, Raff. The only thing to bring me peace is knowing that she's with Dad."

As the two of them share fond memories, my gaze meets Dalton's. He stares back at me with the same smug look on his face he had at the meeting, as if he's won, and all I can do is imagine the things I would do to him if we weren't in a crowd of people.

The one thing I do know is that this is *far* from over.

I SETTLE ONTO THE couch, exhausted from the events of today. While Raff was eager to come inside and discuss the future of his children, or lack thereof, I wasn't having it. I told him that as much as I respect him, his opinion is not something I'm willing to take into consideration. They're grown adults who made their decisions, and now they have to face the consequences for their actions.

Beni sits on the other side of the L-shaped couch and watches as I put my feet up on the coffee table. He's been watching me carefully all day, as if I'm dynamite with a lit fuse, just waiting to explode and wreak havoc on everything around me. And I can't blame him for it, because that's exactly how I feel.

"So, where are we?" I ask. "Anything I should be aware of?"

His brows raise. "You really want to do this now? Today?"

"*Especially* today. What have you found?"

I can see the hesitation in his eyes. He doesn't think we should be discussing this today, and the fact that I want to move on as if we didn't come home from a funeral is concerning him. But I will not stop until Viola is at the same depth of the coffin we put in the ground today.

He sighs and reluctantly pulls out his phone. "The

tracking from Viola's phone hasn't been on since the night of the shooting, but it has helped in seeing her actions that night. She went from the gym to Mari Vanna. From there she waited a couple hours and then came here, which is when Paolo was killed. And then she went home, where—"

I hold up a hand to stop him. He doesn't need to continue. The events of that night will forever be burned into my brain. I don't need a replay of that.

"And what about Nico?" I ask.

He shrugs. "No one has seen or heard from him since the hospital. I'm sure wherever he is, he's hiding out with Viola. Did Raff give you any intel this morning?"

A dry laugh forces itself out of me. "All he did was try to get me to believe she wasn't behind this. He'll never do anything that could harm his precious spawn." I exhale slowly as I feel myself getting worked up. "I don't know. We may need to reevaluate his position in the Familia."

Beni purses his lips but when he glances behind me, he smiles. "Hey, Kamikaze. Dead looks good on you."

My breath hitches, and I turn my head to find Saxon standing there. Her black hair is tied up into a messy bun, and she's clearly lost at least fifteen pounds—from her refusal to eat—but it's still her. She glances over at me but then quickly looks away, a pained look etched on her face.

"You shouldn't be out of bed," I tell her softly.

She scoffs. "What are you going to do? Lock me in there again?"

Giving me no chance to respond, she goes into the kitchen and grabs a bottle of water out of the fridge. It's one thing she's been doing ever since we brought her back here. She knows damn well all she would have to do is ask and I'd bring her one, but since she woke up, she seems to want nothing to do with me.

Without sparing another glance in my direction, she

heads back to her room, and I hear the door click shut. Once we're alone, Beni exhales slowly.

"Damn," he says. "That made *me* feel cold."

I can feel my patience dwindling by the second, and he may have had a point. Today is not the day for this. I get up from my place on the couch, mumbling to Beni that I'm going to lay down. He knows when to come get me.

Before disappearing into my room, I look down the hallway that leads to Saxon's, feeling the same pain in my chest I get every time I think about what we lost. Because while she may not be dead, we may as well be dead to each other.

Chapter 5

Saxon

Have you ever felt pain so bad it knocks the wind out of you? Like literally steals the breath straight from your lungs. It's brutal and unforgiving, making you wonder if you'll ever make it out alive.

That's how I've felt since the moment I woke up after being shot.

The TV Kage mounted on the wall plays some movie that at one point in time I may have found interesting, but now, it's simply background noise. I'm too lost in the depths of despair, drowning in the emptiness that makes me feel like dying every second of the day. The only place I can find solitude is when I'm asleep.

When I can be back with my baby in my dreams.

A knock on the door pulls me from my dark thoughts. As I turn my head, a home nurse comes in—the one requirement Kage had to fulfill in order for the hospital to let him take me home. After all, you can't fake your death and still stay in a public hospital.

She looks nice, with her light blue scrubs and overly

cheery smile. Her hair is piled on top of her head in a messy bun, and she looks well rested and optimistic, but I'm sure if I got inside her mind, I'd see that she's miserable, just like the rest of the world.

No one is really as happy as they pretend to be.

"Hi," she greets me sweetly. "I've just got to change your bandages and check how you're healing, and then I'll be out of your hair."

To be honest, I'd like nothing less right now, because no amount of physical healing will change the fact that I'm mentally and emotionally dead inside. Still, I sigh and nod, letting her know that it's okay for her to do what she's hired to come here for.

She places her bag on the dresser and takes out the needed supplies before coming closer to me. I keep my eyes focused on the TV as she lifts my shirt. She carefully pulls the bandage away, and while I refuse to look at it, I can tell she's happy with the results by how she sighs in relief.

"When was your last surgery?"

I rack my brain for the answer, since all the days seem to blend together. "Four days ago, I think."

There were three surgeries in total. Two were in the same day, but the last was shortly before I was discharged. By the time I left the hospital, it was without a spleen, an appendix, and most importantly, my son.

She smiles. "It's healing slowly, but well. Another week and you should be able to get these stitches out."

"Great," I drone.

Grabbing the antiseptic, she goes to pour it onto a couple pieces of gauze when it slips out of her hand and splashes all over my bed. The cold liquid soaks both me and my bedsheets.

"Oh!" she yelps. "I'm so sorry. Please, let me help you up so I can get this cleaned up for you."

She holds her hands out for me to take, but I swat them

away and stand by myself. She may mean well, but I'm tired of people treating me like I'm fragile. I'm not. I simply don't want to fucking be here. Or anywhere, for that matter.

The sheets are stripped from my bed, and the nurse runs out to retrieve new ones and a towel to dry the mattress. As I'm left alone, I roll my eyes, catching the mirror in my peripheral vision.

The girl looking back at me is someone I don't recognize.

She's bitter.

She's cold.

She's full of spite and vengeful rage.

My gaze travels down to where my shirt is still tucked up under my bra. Since I left the hospital, my incisions have been constantly covered by bandages, and I never had the courage to look beneath them. But now, they're on full display.

My eyes lock onto the marks that ruined me.

The pinkish scars that show where the bullets ripped through my flesh and embedded themselves in my body, killing my baby before he even got a chance to live.

I feel as my blood starts to boil. Wrath seeps up my body, coiling around my lungs. It's suffocating. My heart pounds against my ribcage as my breathing becomes labored. My fingernails dig into the palms of my hands and my vision starts to blur. A hazy fog clouds my mind in fiery violence, flipping a switch and sending me into a blind rage.

And the last thing I remember before it all goes dark is picking up my desk chair and throwing it full force into the mirror.

CHAPTER 6

KAGE

My bedroom door flies open, waking me from a restless slumber and throwing me back into the grim reality I've found myself in. Beni stands in the doorway with a wide-eyed look on his face, and before he can even begin to tell me what's wrong, I hear the crash.

I'm on my feet in an instant, running toward Saxon's room. The nurse stands outside the door with a frightened look on her face, and she flinches as the sound of something else breaking comes from the bedroom. Without hesitation, I push open the door and my jaw locks as I see the state that Saxon is in.

She stares back at me but there's nothing in her eyes that resembles the woman she once was. Her shirt is raised, and the blood that covers her stomach tells me she ripped her stitches and reopened her wounds.

Her room is in shambles. The TV is hanging from where it was securely mounted to the wall. The mirror and the desk chair are in pieces, and her bed is flipped over. Even the drawers are pulled from the dresser and thrown across the room.

I take a step inside, watching her carefully for any sudden movements. Instead, she stays completely still, looking like a caged animal ready to attack when threatened. Out of all the possibilities I thought could happen, being *afraid* of her next move never even crossed my mind, and yet here we are.

"S," I say calmly. "You're hurt. We have to get you cleaned up."

"Fuck you," she sneers.

Crossing the room quicker than she was ready for, I grab her wrists and pin her up against the wall—my own anger seeping through. "Oh, Gabbana. I *have* fucked you. And you fucking loved it."

She keeps her head held high as she glares back at me, and no matter how much she may hate me now, I can still feel it. The sexual tension that crackles between us, there's no getting rid of it. And goddamn, I've gone too long without feeling her mouth on mine.

I don't know if it's because I can't resist anymore, or because I'm desperate to calm her down, but I drop my head down and press my lips to hers. There, in the middle of destruction, I kiss her like she's breathing the life back into me. Like we're breathing the life back into each other. It's an intoxicating dose of serotonin straight to my system, until the pain comes in.

She bites down on my lip hard enough for the metallic taste of blood to hit my tastebuds. I hiss as I release her and pull away, only to feel her drive her knee full force between my legs. My balls contract, tightening so hard it feels like someone is trying to squeeze them like their own personal stress ball. Bile rises in my throat as I empty all the air in my lungs and drop down to one knee.

"That wasn't very nice," I growl.

Saxon looks down at me, smirking triumphantly, but she

hasn't won yet. I pull the syringe from my pocket and remove the cap before driving it into the side of her thigh. Her breath hitches as I push the plunger down and inject the sedative into her bloodstream.

My own pain be damned, I get up and catch her before she falls, instantly going to sleep. Beni and the nurse watch me as I carry her out of the room and down the hall.

"Get me Dr. Ferro," I order Beni. "She's going to need new stitches."

"On it, Boss," he answers.

Taking her into my room, I lie her down on the bed and sit beside her. My fingers gently push the little strands of hair out of her face as I take in how peaceful she looks. As if pain isn't the only thing she's capable of feeling.

The girl I know is in there somewhere.

I just have to find her.

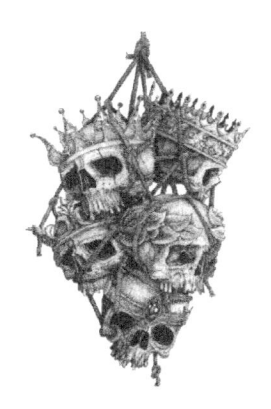

EVERYONE HAS THEIR ESCAPES. Some like reading books, while others would rather go for a run. Mine, however, are always violent. Whether it's getting revenge on my enemies or throwing punches in the gym, the only things that can get through to me are those that inflict pain.

The drills Ralph has me running are the same as always,

except this time it feels different. All my anger and frustration is being taken out on the focus mitts he's holding. Each hit is harder than the last as I drive my fists into the padding, craving the release.

The time Saxon spent in the hospital, including during the first and second surgeries that literally saved her life twice, all I wanted was for her to wake up. For her to be okay. And she did, she woke up. But okay isn't a word I'd use to describe her.

Immediately, she was different.

Cold.

Enraged.

Ready to burn the whole world to the ground.

But while I understand the grudge she holds, it never occurred to me that she would hate me, too. Every part of me is ready to fight. To stand by her side and refuse to let any harm come to her as we punish those who did this to her. But she seems determined to let the pain and the misery break her down to nothing. And *that* is the fear that haunts me at night.

Because I saw the same look on my mother before she took her own life.

MY FINGERS MOVE ACROSS the keyboard, searching everywhere I know to check for any signs of Viola or Nico. I may have nothing yet, but I can feel it. We're getting closer. It's only a matter of time before we close in on both of them, and I can fire two bullets straight into their skulls.

I have half a mind to drag Viola back here when I find her. To let Saxon drive one of her heels straight into her eyeball and listen as she screams in pure agony. But to do that would mean showing Saxon a life of blood and violence, and it's a dangerous slope. Once you've felt the power of inflicting pain on someone else, of taking someone's life, there's no coming back from it. You end up feening for it like an addict looking for their next fix.

My office door opens and slams shut with a force that shakes the walls. I look up to find a very angry Saxon glaring back at me. I lean back in my seat, giving her all of my attention, but it's as effective as that kiss was earlier. With the vindictive look in her eyes, I wouldn't be surprised if she was plotting my murder.

"You fucking drugged me again," she growls.

I keep my emotions calm. "You should have listened."

"Oh!" she scoffs. "Because God forbid I don't do what you want. Have you *ever* had a relationship where you don't call all the shots?"

"Is that what this is? A relationship?" I question. "And to answer your question, no. I haven't, and I'm sure as hell not starting now if it means standing by while you kill yourself!"

"I'm already dead!" Her voice echoes around the room while her words hit me straight in the chest. "Don't you get that? The funeral you went to may as well have been real!"

I'm out of my seat and shaking my head. "Don't say that."

"Why? Because you know it's true?" She's taunting me, and I feel my ire rising to the surface. "I don't want to live anymore! I don't want to live knowing my baby died!"

Maybe it's the fear, or the bottled up emotions when it

comes to the pregnancy, but it all explodes inside of me. My restraint snaps as my fist clenches at my side.

"Our baby!" I roar. "Our baby died! I lost that baby too!"

She rolls her eyes and looks away as I get closer. "Right, and I'm sure you're so broken up about it."

I cage her in against the wall and slam my fist next to her head. "Don't. Don't do that. It's fucking killing me inside."

"Says the guy who got a vasectomy at eighteen years old because he didn't want to have kids."

It's a dig, and one I expected, but it still hits its target as I crack a little more.

"I don't!" I shout. "Or at least I didn't, until…"

"Until what?" Putting her hands on my chest, she uses all her strength to push me away. "Spit it out!"

"Until you!" My words make her flinch. "Until I found out that having a family with you was a fucking possibility." She huffs and shakes her head, focusing her attention on the floor. "But I guess that's dead, too, with the way you can barely even look at me."

Finally, her eyes meet mine, and the pain I see in them threatens to break my cold, black heart. Saxon is one of the strongest women I know, and to see her in such mental anguish—it's devastating.

"I don't look at you because it hurts." Her voice trembles as the walls she has put up to keep everyone out start to crumble. "Because every time I see you, every time I look into your eyes…"

A sob rips through her, followed by another one, making her unable to finish the sentence, but she doesn't need to. I get it. For the first time since she woke up, I fucking get it.

I wrap my arms around her as she breaks down completely, letting out all of the agony she's been holding inside. Tears flow from her eyes, and she pulls at everything she can. Her hair, my suit, her shirt, my neck. It's destroying her. Ripping her apart until there's nothing left, and all I can do is hold her through it.

Rubbing my hand up and down her back, I feel myself enduring the same pain she is as I whisper that I've got her. That she's going to be okay. And I pray to a God I don't believe in, that what I'm saying is true.

MY BACK RESTS AGAINST the wall, with Saxon lying on the floor. Her head is in my lap as I run my fingers through her hair. It took a while for her to get through the breakdown that tore through her body like a tornado, but we got her there. Together.

She looks up at me with a tired look on her face, and a hint of a smile seeps through. "I got to meet him, you know. Our baby."

"You did?"

She nods. "I think it was when I was in surgery. The first one."

A million things run through my mind at once, including the sickening realization that I almost lost her, but I smile softly back at her. "Tell me about him."

And she does. For hours we lie there, talking about how he had my eyes and her smile, and imagining what our life would have been like with a miniature us running around and wreaking havoc on the world. She talks about him with such love and passion that I start to see sparks of the girl I thought I lost forever. And when we both fall asleep right there on the floor of my office, I dream of the little boy with Saxon's dimples.

CHAPTER 7

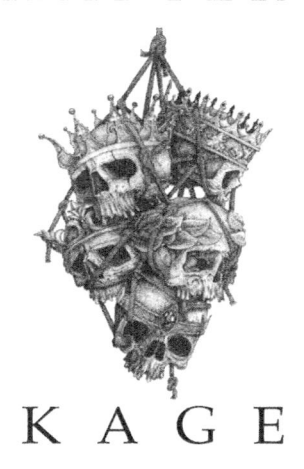

KAGE

Screams fill the room, bouncing off the walls and sounding like music to my ears. A Bratva hangs his head, with his wrists and ankles cuffed to the wall in front of me. He's at my mercy and he fucking knows it.

"Tell me where she is," I demand.

Blood drips from the wound as he groans in pain. "I told you. I don't know who you're talking about, but even if I did, I wouldn't tell you."

Dropping my knife, I clench my fist and punch him as hard as I can across the face. "Wrong fucking answer, shithead."

We managed to grab this Bratva scumbag outside of the gym Viola was at the day Saxon was shot. I had Roman and Cesari running surveillance on it to see if Viola showed her face again. She's not entirely stupid, but she *is* vain. But while there were no signs of Viola, this prick was seen hanging around as if he was waiting for someone. When he finally went to leave, Cesari grabbed him.

"I already know she switched sides," I sneer in his face.

"Just tell me where she is, and I won't pull your fucking teeth out and make you swallow them."

He spits blood at my feet. "Fuck you, Italian scum."

I chuckle, always finding it comical when they act tough despite being nothing but weak little bitches. Walking over to the thick chain that sits in a pile on the ground, I pick it up and fold it in half, holding it tightly in my hand.

"I suggest you tell me where she is, or you're about to feel pain that'll make everything before this feel like a tickle."

His throat bobs with a heavy swallow as he stares at the chain. "I swear to God, I don't know who you're talking about."

"I don't fucking buy it," I say as I whip the chain across his side. "Where is she?"

He roars in pain, taking a minute to catch his breath. "Fuck!"

"Come on." I press. "Give up the little bitch and the pain stops. It's as simple as that." He doesn't say anything so I whip him again. "I've got nothing better to do. I can make this last all fucking day."

As I lift the chain again, he breaks. "Okay, okay." He pauses to take a few breaths. "Describe her for me. They've all got their bitches."

"Thin. Brown hair. Wealthy. Stuck up princess with boundary issues."

He scoffs. "Oh, yeah. That narrows it down to about half of Manhattan."

"Fucking prick! She goes to the gym you were seen hanging around!" What little patience I have is wearing thin and fast. "She shot and killed the daughter of Dalton Forbes on his orders."

A smile makes its way to his face. "Ah, you mean Forbes's bitch. The one hanging on his arm all the damn time."

My eyes widen. "Dalton is fucking Viola?"

"If that's her name, sure," he says carelessly. "I'm not close with him. I've just seen those two together a lot."

The thought of Viola sleeping with Dalton is vomit inducing. Dalton has done far worse shit, so the fact that he's having an affair doesn't surprise me. What *does* shock me, however, is the fact that it's with Viola. If Raff finds out, he's going to be livid. And I'm going to make sure he does.

"Ok, now we're getting somewhere," I say, dropping the chain on the ground. "So, where is a place she would hide out?"

"I don't know, man! I told you, we're not close." I bend down to pick up the chain again. "All right, wait."

"You've got five seconds."

He exhales. "There's an apartment in Long Island. We use it as a hideout after shit goes down. It's near the high school. Brick building. Almost looks abandoned. It's apartment 256."

I wrap my hand around his throat and his eyes lock with mine. "You better not be sending me on some wild goose chase, or I swear to God. I'll come back here and whip you with that chain until there isn't a single part of you *not* bleeding."

Letting him go, I turn around and leave the shed. Beni follows behind me and locks the doors shut. I used to make it a rule not to bring anyone back to my house. It's too predictable. But these days, I can't bring myself to leave Saxon. While she's been progressively improving since her breakdown, she still has her rough days.

"Pull the Escalade into the garage," I tell Beni as we cross the backyard. "I'll meet you in there."

He nods and heads that way, while I head to my bedroom. I grab a hat and a hoodie out of my closet and then go find Saxon. She's sitting on the couch, reading a book, when I toss both items in front of her.

"Put those on," I tell her. "We have somewhere to be."

She looks down at the pitiful disguise and then back up at

me like I've lost my mind. "Uh, are you forgetting that I'm supposed to be dead? Isn't that risky?"

"Definitely, but if you think I'm leaving you here, you're mistaken. Let's go."

With a roll of her eyes, she gets up. I grab the hat and put it on her head before wrapping the hoodie around her, making sure her hair is tucked inside of it. She looks up at me through her lashes as I pull the hood up, and I can't resist pressing a kiss to the top of her head.

"You ready?" I ask.

She grabs her book off of the couch. "No, but you're the boss."

I chuckle at her sarcasm and take her hand in mine. "You bet your ass I am."

THROUGHOUT THE WHOLE RIDE to Long Island, Saxon stays quiet. She's curled up into a ball in the backseat, keeping her head down and reading her book. She was right when she said that bringing her out in public is risky. If Dalton gets word that she's still alive, there's no doubt in my mind that he'll come after her again. One thing's for sure: I've never been more thankful for blacked-out windows.

"I think this is it," I tell Beni as he pulls into the parking lot.

The shithead was right. This place looks like it hasn't been lived in by anyone with an income over $15k a year. The grass out front hasn't been cut all season and most of the windows have plywood in place of the broken glass. While I can see why the Bratva hide out here, it seems too low class for Princess Viola.

I hop out of the car and take three steps toward the apartment when I hear another car door close. I turn around to see Beni following behind me. Putting up one hand, I stop him.

"Stay here with her," I tell him. "I've got this."

He leans against the car. "All right, but call if you need me."

"Will do."

It takes a few minutes, but I manage to find apartment 256. It's upstairs, overlooking the empty pool filled with greenish rain water and garbage. Homeless people are clearly using the small amount of cover as shelter, and battered shopping carts filled with all kinds of things are scattered in the hallways.

I listen for any sounds coming from inside the apartment but hear nothing. The curtains are shut on the windows, giving me no chance but to go in blind. I pull my gun out and rear back, kicking the door right off the hinges. Pieces of the door jamb fly into the apartment, but there's still no sign of anyone.

I step inside, carefully looking around before I move down the hallway. Mattresses covered in stains lie on the floor of each bedroom, and the only inkling that the Bratva prick wasn't lying about this place are the knives and burner phone found in one of the kitchen drawers. But there's no sign of Viola, and if I had to guess, only the lower members of the Bratva use this place.

Walking back to the car, I see Beni calmly smoking a cigarette. He exhales out a cloud as I get closer.

"No luck?"

I shake my head. "Not in that shithole."

He huffs. "So, back to home base to torture some more information out of him?"

"Nah," I answer. "Let's go to Raff's; let him know what a traitorous slut his little princess really is. Maybe then he'll give her up. And where there's Viola, I'm sure there will be Nico."

Climbing into the car, I find myself getting angry as I think about how she's managed to stay in hiding for two weeks now. Someone has to be helping her, and so help me God, if it's Raff, his days in the Familia are done.

I glance at the back seat to find Saxon sleeping soundly. Her book rests in her lap while her head leans against the door. It's the one of the few times I get to see her looking like she isn't battling a million demons.

Beni hops in the driver's seat and puts the car in drive, pulling my attention away from Saxon and back to the road.

I'm going to find this little bitch if it's the last thing I do.

RAFF'S HOUSE IS A place that used to feel safe. Never

like home, but safe nonetheless. But lately, I feel like I need to have my guard up around him. Despite all the times he has insisted that we are family, he knows right now I'm after his *actual* family. There's no doubt in my mind that he would choose the twins over me, any day of the week.

Knocking on the door, I wait for the sound of footsteps, but they never come. I glance over at where Raff's car sits in the driveway—the only car he has. The man has always insisted on driving everywhere, even when it was only his wife's errands. So, if he expects me to believe he's not home, he's really underestimating how much I pay attention to detail.

"Go wait in the car," I tell Beni, knowing this conversation won't take place on the porch like I had planned.

His shoulders slump in disappointment that he won't get to see Raff's reaction when I tell him about Viola's recent bedroom activities, but he obeys while I pull the key from my pocket. Sticking it into the lock, I open the door and step inside. The whole place is quiet and mostly empty, except for Raff, who is sitting at the kitchen table reading a newspaper.

He looks up and pretends to startle when he sees me. "Kage!"

My brows raise. "You didn't hear me knocking?"

Putting the newspaper down, he shakes his head. "My hearing isn't all that great these days. Getting old is a bitch, son."

"Why is this the first I'm hearing about it? Have you gone to see a doctor?"

"So they can put one of those screeching hearing aids in my ear?" He waves off the idea. "I'd rather go deaf."

I nod and take a seat across from him at the table while he gets up and pours me a cup of coffee, even though it's the middle of the damn day. As he places it on the table in front of me, I notice it's in the same mug I've used since I lived here. My father's favorite.

"Good to see your memory is intact," I quip.

He snorts. "Give it time."

Putting the coffee pot back on the warmer, he brings me the sugar and the cream and then sits back in his seat.

"So, what've you been up to boy?"

I stir my coffee with the spoon and then lift it to take a sip. "Managed to get ahold of a Bratva. Roman and Cesari snatched him up outside of a gym this morning. He's proven to be rather useful."

"A *useful* Bratva?" he scoffs. "Impossible."

Leaning back, I rest my ankle on my knee. "He gave me some information I think you'd be keen to know."

That grabs his attention and his brows raise. "Did he now? And what would that be?"

"Seems Viola's traitor status goes well beyond shooting Saxon. She's been fucking Dalton."

Raff sputters on air. "Absolutely not. You can't actually believe that garbage."

"Why not?" I argue. "You said yourself, if she did this, it was on someone else's orders. Dalton made it very clear at that meeting that he knew about the hit out on his daughter."

"And *you* said she did it because she wants you," he counters. "These are very conflicting stories."

I throw my hands in the air. "Why does it matter *why* she did it? She. Killed. Saxon. You know, Saxon. Silas's granddaughter, that you were so adamant on keeping safe, even from me. Guess that only applies to those who are your flesh and blood."

His eyes roll, showing he's getting frustrated with this conversation. "Don't start that. I'm not picking sides here. The three of you are *all* my children."

My body tenses as I start to get heated, but just before I open my mouth to respond, the ceiling above us creeks. It's not loud by any means, but it catches both of our attention. I watch Raff carefully as he glances quickly at the ceiling.

"Funny. You can't hear a knock on the front door but you can hear that."

Within seconds we're both out of our seats. I'm taking the stairs two at a time while Raff follows behind me, begging me to stop. He's blabbering on about house-settling noises, but I won't hear it. I march down the hallway and into the bedroom that used to be my own. It's the only room directly above the kitchen.

A desk sits against the far wall, covered in paperwork of Raff's. There's a filing cabinet beside it with a chair and lamp in the corner, but otherwise it looks empty. Except...

I pull out my gun and aim it at the closet, firing one shot straight through the door. A loud scream comes from inside, while Nico roars in pain.

"Fuck!"

Feeling the betrayal deep in my soul, I glare at Raff. "Get them the fuck out of there, *now*."

His eyes water in fear. "Kage. Don't do this."

I cock the gun and point it at the closet door again. "Now!"

The closet door opens and Viola saunters out, looking like she's been very well taken care of over the last couple weeks. Behind her, Nico looks the same, except for the bullet that grazed his arm. Raff immediately rushes over to him when he sees the bleeding, but my attention is locked on the bitch who killed my baby.

"Please don't do this," Viola cries.

I scoff. "What's wrong? Can give it but can't take it?"

Nico hisses as Raff ties a ripped T-shirt around his arm. "Kage, he needs stitches."

"He needs nothing but a fucking body bag," I snap. "He had his orders, and he knew what would happen if he didn't obey them."

"She didn't do it!" Nico yells.

I move the gun from Viola to him. "I wasn't speaking to you!"

Viola starts to sob. "He's telling the truth. I swear on everything, Kage. I didn't kill Saxon!"

"Bullshit!" I growl. "I saw the tracking on your phone. It was at the crime scene when she was shot!"

"I was at the gym and someone attacked me from behind," she cries. "They put something over my mouth and next thing I knew, I was waking up hours later in my car. Someone is framing me!"

"Then why run? Why hide?"

She looks at me as if the answer is obvious. "Because I woke up to find out that my house was burned to the ground and the girl you were fucking crazy about was in the hospital with two gunshot wounds. And when Nico found me, I knew I was being accused of it."

If there's one thing I've learned about Viola, it's that she should've been an actress. The little psychopath knows exactly how to play on emotions and she does it well, which is why I'm not buying this. She simply underestimated my feelings for Saxon and what I would do for her.

I move my gun slightly to the right and fire a shot through the wall. Raff and Nico both flinch while Viola screams my name.

"I don't fucking buy it!" I roar. You wanted her gone! You made no secret of that!"

Pointing the gun right at her head, I watch as a tear streams down her face. She's stopped panicking, now accepting her fate. She's going to die today."

"This is for Saxon *and* my baby."

My finger begins to press on the trigger when Saxon bolts into the room, putting herself in between Viola and me.

"Kage, stop!"

Raff, Nico, and Viola all freeze at the sight of a ghost.

"You're alive?" Nico shouts, seeming relieved by the new revelation, but it changes nothing.

"Move, Sax," I order.

Beni tries to pull her away, but she fights him off. "No. You're not doing this. Not to them."

My rage is only getting worse with the realization that Viola now knows that Saxon is still alive. "She tried to kill you! She deserves to die!"

Saxon's breathing quickens. "She didn't!"

I'm frantically looking for any way to shoot her without potentially shooting Saxon, but there isn't one. I need her to move. "I saw the evidence! Get the fuck out of my way!"

"Kage, you're not hearing me!" she yells in a panic. "She didn't do it! It wasn't her!"

"How can you be so sure?"

Saxon's shoulders sag. "Because I know who did!"

My arm falls to my side, an unwelcome confusion creeping in. "Well, care to share with the fucking class?"

She takes three steps towards me, putting her hands on my chest. "No, because this isn't your battle. It's mine."

Viola falls to the ground, finally being able to breathe, while Nico and Raff both exhale in relief. But they're far from off the hook themselves. Viola may be innocent, but Nico disobeyed direct orders and Raff made his stance very clear when he chose to hide them from me.

"Go get that stitched up, and then I want the two of you at my place," I tell them both. "There are things we need to discuss."

They both nod and leave the room as my eyes lock with Viola's. She stares back at me with unadulterated fear, obviously afraid that I'll change my mind and fire a bullet right between her eyes, but Saxon grabs my arm and leads me out of the room before I can. And if the sobs she lets out when I'm gone are anything to go by, the message is clear—Saxon is untouchable.

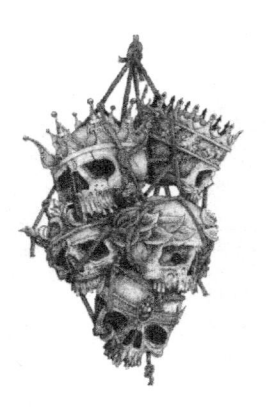

THE THREE OF US sit in the car, with Saxon back to gazing out the window while Beni drives. I glance back at her, but she won't meet my eyes. As I turn back around, I run my fingers through my hair.

"You're really not going to tell me who shot you?" I ask, exasperated.

She doesn't answer, but I catch a single tear sliding down her face in the rearview mirror.

I wrack my brain to try to figure out who it could be. Not only did they have to shoot Saxon, but they had to kill Paolo in order to get her out of the house. I've seen the video of Paolo's murder, and it was definitely a woman. Most women don't have it in them to slit someone's throat, nor do they have the strength to put a man in that position, but Viola does. Which is why I was so convinced it was her. But someone went through great lengths to make us believe that, and we almost played right into their hand.

"What do you want to do about the Bratva in the shed?" Beni asks. "Dispose of him?"

I run my hand over the facial hair that covers my chin. "Leave him. He doesn't handle pain well and sings like a canary. He may be of use to us."

Chapter 8

Saxon

Most people run from the darkness. They fear it in a way that makes it hard to rationalize what's real and what's not. After all, it's where all the monsters and demons come to play. I, however, embrace it. My demons wrap their arms around me and rock me to sleep at night while the darkness hovers, bending down to kiss my forehead. They bring me peace and protect me from my damage.

I gaze out my bedroom window, my eyes focused on the shed in the back corner. I'd seen Kage and Beni go in and out of there a few times, but it never really occurred to me what could be in there until now. Overhearing them talk about someone being in there grabbed my attention and held it in a vise, and now I can't stop my mind from going deeper and deeper into what that part of Kage's life is like.

A knock on my bedroom door yanks my attention away from the window, and I stare at the TV as if I've been grossly absorbed into *My 600lb Life* this whole time. As the door creaks as it opens, I glance over to see Viola peeking her head in. She smiles shyly at me, which is definitely not a good look for her.

"Mind if I come in?"

I tilt my head to the side. "Why? Want to finish the job you started?"

Her eyes widen as she runs inside and shuts the door behind her. "Oh my God, that's not funny. Kage will shoot me in the head if he hears you say that."

"Maybe that's my intention."

She crosses her arms over her chest. "I wasn't the one who shot you, and we both know that."

I snort. "No, but that doesn't mean you're not a royal pain in my ass."

"That's actually why I'm here." She comes over and sits on the edge of the bed. "I think you and I got off on the wrong foot."

Cocking a single brow at her, I hum. "Is that right?"

"It is," she says. "I formed an opinion before I got a chance to know the real you, and that was wrong of me. After all, you can't be all that bad. You didn't let Kage kill me."

"I still might," I drawl and take a sip of my wine.

A heavy sigh flows from her mouth as she moves closer. "I want to make it up to you."

This has to be a joke. She may not have been the one to shoot me, but the Viola I know would have danced on my grave. Still, I bite, because I'm curious.

"And how do you plan on doing that?"

She grins. "By being your friend, duh."

I choke on air, the whole idea being outlandish. "Yeah, hard pass. Thanks anyway."

This is the girl who wants nothing more than to push me away from Kage. She's underestimating me if she thinks I've grown up in a world where the motto isn't *keep your friends close and your enemies closer*.

"Oh, come on," she presses. "According to the world, you're dead. I'd imagine that gets pretty lonely."

The corner of my mouth raises. "Don't worry. I have Kage."

She makes a sound of disgust. "Is that what this is about? Honey, he held a gun to my head. The part of me that thought he and I have a future together went up in flames when he spent two straight weeks hunting me down like a fox in the woods. Believing that man's future is with anyone but you would be idiotic."

Well, at least she's a little more grounded in reality than before, but I'm still not about to sign up for Team Viola. "Seriously, thanks, but no thanks. I'm perfectly content here in my little bubble."

With a finger to her lips, she looks me over like she's considering my words. "Hmm. Nope. I'm going to win you over, Saxon Forbes. You'll see. Trust me."

I look her in the eyes and speak with the most sincerity I've ever had in my life. "I don't trust anyone."

"You will," she says, not taking no for an answer.

THE TWO OF US sit in an awkward silence for over an hour. I stare at the TV while Viola scrolls on her phone, trying to show me a couple funny memes or talking shit about what some celebrity was seen wearing out last night.

And personally, I don't give a shit if Brad and Jennifer had some epic reunion in front of the whole world, but she sure does.

Kage comes into the room and freezes when he sees Viola sitting next to me on the bed, and within seconds, his hand is on the blade he keeps in his pocket. His eyes move from mine to hers, and I hear as her breath hitches. She really is afraid of him, and the thought of that makes me happier than it should.

"Out," he orders Viola.

She scrambles off of the bed and makes her way out the door like a child who was just caught with their hands in the cookie jar. Meanwhile, Kage makes his way over to me.

"Are you okay? Did she hurt you?"

I hum. "If I say yes, will you make sure she never comes back?"

"Yes," he answers seriously. "Just say the word. Whatever you want."

It's tempting, really. The thought of Viola trying to be my friend makes my skin crawl. If I'm being honest, there isn't a single thing I find likable about that woman. But killing her means making a mess for Kage when it comes to Nico and Raff, and I just don't find getting rid of her to be worth that.

"It's fine," I tell him. "She was just trying to thank me for saving her life."

He takes his suit jacket off and goes to hang it in the closet. "I'm still not entirely sure why you did."

Since I destroyed my own room, I've been permanently moved to the master with Kage. And before you think of all the X-rated things that could be happening, let me tell you—they're not. There's no denying that he cares about me. He's made that crystal clear with the way he's willing to literally kill for me. But he's also been treating me like I'm made of glass; as if one wrong move will shatter me into a million pieces. And maybe he's right, or maybe I just need him to grab me by my throat and take fucking charge.

"Honestly? Me either," I tell him as he strips down to his boxers and gets into bed.

He chuckles as he leans over and presses a kiss to my forehead. "Well, tomorrow we're going to talk about who it is that shot you. I refuse to live in a world where they get to exist without consequences."

My mind goes back to that night.

The excruciating pain that ripped through my abdomen.

The heat from the fire making it hard to breathe.

The sound of her heels clicking across the floor as she left me there for dead is burned into my mind, playing on an endless loop and haunting me in my darkest nightmares.

My death should've irrevocably changed her life. She should be in an inconsolable state of grief, and yet, she's the one that caused it. And I can't help but wonder if she feels even the slightest ounce of guilt when she sees pictures of me hanging on the wall or watches as Kylie mourns the loss of her big sister.

"Oh, she won't go without consequences," I promise him. "But they'll be delivered at my hands, not yours. And when the time comes, it'll be *me* who avenges our baby."

BEING THE PERSISTENT SHIT she is, I should've

known to take Viola at her word. For the next three days, she's by my side. Sucking up isn't her specialty, that much is obvious, but she does her best. And when she brings a case of wine because Kage locked me out of the wine cellar...well, I don't entirely hate her that day.

"I'm not saying Elena should've chosen Stefan," she argues as she tosses a piece of popcorn into her mouth. "I'm just saying she should've taken advantage of the golden opportunity for a grade-A threesome."

That's the first thing she's said that pulls a laugh out of me. "So you're Team Damon then?"

She scoffs. "Hell no. I'm strictly Team Kai. Have you *seen* that man's smirk? Come to mama."

Chuckling, I take a sip of my wine, but I don't miss the way she looks my way and smirks. My brows raise as I start to wonder if she's completely lost her mind, or she's plotting another way to get rid of me.

"What?" I ask.

She shrugs and turns back to the TV. "I told you I'd win you over."

I roll my eyes. "You're not the complete worst."

Her lips purse. "I'll take it."

Kage walks in, stopping to glare at the glasses of wine in each of our hands. Viola keeps her eyes locked on the screen. I can't tell if she still hasn't recovered from him damn near shooting her in the head, or if she genuinely just doesn't care what he thinks. Honestly, it's probably a little of both. I, however, give him my sweetest smile.

His nostrils flare as he goes into the kitchen and yanks the refrigerator door open. He grabs a beer and lightly slams the door shut before marching back toward his office.

"Fucking Mancini twins, stealing her attention," he grumbles under his breath.

Once he's gone, my eyes lock with Viola's and we both break out into hysterical laughter. She damn near spills her wine, she's laughing so hard. And when she finally manages to compose herself, she presses a hand to her chest.

"My God. I've never seen him pout like such a toddler before," she says in disbelief.

My brows raise, but before I can open my mouth, a letter opener flies through the air—just missing Viola's head and sticking itself into the wall. Her eyes widen as she turns around to see Kage standing there, practically shooting lasers from his eyes.

"Right," she murmurs. "Well, that's my cue."

She stands up and grabs her purse, going into the kitchen to empty her glass of wine. When she's done, she turns to look at me and smiles.

"I'll see you later, S."

I nod. "Yeah, sure."

The second she's out the door, Kage is already heading toward me. "What the fuck was that, S?"

It takes everything in my power to hold back my smile, amused with how possessive he is. "I don't know. She's determined to become my friend."

"And you're okay with that?"

I shrug half-heartedly. "She's…tolerable. And besides, it's not like I can go out and find new friends, being dead and all."

He stares back at me before shaking his head. "No. Nope. I don't like it."

Giggling, I stand up and walk toward him, dipping my fingers into his pockets. "I can't spend the rest of my life with just you and Beni."

He cocks a single brow at me. "Who the fuck said Beni is invited?"

"Kage," I laugh. "I need other friends."

"Why?"

Arching up on my tippy-toes, I press a kiss over his heart.

"Because they keep me from wanting to kill you in your sleep."

His hands land on my arms, and he moves me away from him so he can look down at me. "How many times have you considered doing that exactly?"

"Four…"

"Oh," he says, relieved.

"…teen."

Sputtering on air, his jaw drops. "Fourteen?"

I tilt my head side to side. "Give or take a few."

"Saxon!" he groans, his amusement slipping through.

"What?" I ask innocently. "You're a little insufferable sometimes."

The corners of his mouth raise as he stares down at me. "Mm-hm. Great. I'm sleeping in the panic room from now on."

A laugh bubbles out of me as I press my lips to his. "That's probably smart."

THE NEXT DAY IS a bad one. The kind where I wouldn't mind if my bed wanted to swallow me whole and take me away from the pains and hardships of being alive. Kage watches me carefully, trying to get me to eat and making sure I have enough fluids, but it's only making me more irritated.

Why can't everyone just leave me alone?

Hell, why couldn't they have just let me die?

Everything I've read said that depression comes in waves, some bigger than others, and that's proven to be true. But today, it's a goddamn tsunami, and I am drowning.

I wrap the blanket around me and sink into the bed, letting the emotions rip their way through me as I sob. It's brutal and relentless, making it hard to breathe at times. I grip at the bed sheets, trying to get the mental pain and anguish to go away, but there's no use.

When Viola comes over, she stands at the door and battles between leaving me be and helping me. Finally, she drops her purse on the floor and climbs onto the bed.

Her arms wrap around me and she goes to pull me close but I fight her off. Still, she doesn't relent. She forces me into her arms and holds me until I stop pushing her away, finally breaking down in her arms. She runs her fingers through my hair as I cry.

I cry for the loss of my baby.

I cry for the loss of the life I had before.

I cry for the betrayal that feels like a blade through the chest.

Kage comes in moments later. He and Viola share a look, and she carefully moves so that Kage can take her place. He kisses my cheek and wipes the tears from my eyes, telling me that I'm not alone.

That he understands.

That he's here.

And it helps. Not enough to stop the pain, but enough to keep me from thinking about the quickest and easiest ways to die.

It keeps me alive.

KAGE CROSSES HIS ARMS over his chest and shakes his head, as if there is no room for negotiation. Viola rolls her eyes, clearly annoyed and thinking he's being unreasonable, while I sit on the couch, curled in a ball and giggling at the two of them.

"No," Kage says for the third time in twenty seconds. "Absolutely not. No."

Four.

Viola scoffs. "Will you just let me—"

"No."

"That's five," I murmur quietly, earning a glare from them both that has me sinking back into my seat.

"You can't keep her cooped up in here!" Viola argues.

He slams his head down on the counter that separates the kitchen and the living room. "You are not taking her shopping, and that's final!"

She stops her foot like an actual child having a tantrum. "Why not?"

"She's supposed to be dead!" he roars. "Dead people don't go shopping!"

"Well, if you'd let me finish, I have a solution for that."

"Oh, this ought to be good."

She puts her purse on the counter and pulls out a brown wig and a pair of oversized sunglasses, holding them up like they're the answer to all the world's problems. "See? No one will know it's her."

I chuckle in amusement while Kage pinches the bridge of his nose. "You've got to be kidding me."

"Shut up," she chastises. "You're the one who stuck a baseball cap and a hoodie on her and called it a disguise."

He takes a deep breath, looking like he's trying to convince himself *not* to *really* kill her this time, and then turns to face her. "Let me make this very clear. Over my dead body will you be risking her life by putting a wig and sunglasses on her and taking her fucking shopping."

"But she's practically fully healed. She can handle herself."

Kage snorts. "I'd hardly call having her stitches removed *last week* fully healed. And besides, this is about her *safety,* not her health."

Viola puts a hand on her hip. "Has anyone ever told you that you suck the fun out of everything?"

He looks back at her, fully fed up with her shit. "Aren't you a little old to be quoting *Freaky Friday*?"

She scrunches her nose and shakes her head. "You're a fun-sucker."

"Really mature. Seriously," he says. "How you don't have a boyfriend is a mystery to me."

Accepting defeat, she gives him a dirty look and plops herself down on the couch beside me. Meanwhile, the door opens and Beni rushes through the door from outside.

"We've got to go," he tells Kage. "I've got intel on where Vladimir is, but we have to act fast."

Kage's eyes widen. "He's back?"

"I'll explain everything in the helicopter. We don't have much time."

Kage runs a hand through his hair, looking conflicted. He clearly doesn't trust Viola worth shit, but when he looks at me, he exhales.

"Go," I tell him. "I'll be okay."

He nods and comes over, covering my mouth with his own in a kiss much more passionate than the cheap things I've been getting recently. When he pulls away, he focuses all his attention on Viola.

"Anything happens to her, and I'll have your head mounted on my wall," he promises.

She says nothing as the helicopter outside starts up and Kage heads to the door where Beni waits.

"How'd you get information on Vlad?" Kage asks.

Beni chuckles. "The little bitch in the shed gave him up for a Snickers."

Kage throws his head back and laughs as he pulls the door closed behind him.

My attention turns to the backyard, seeing the shed that Beni must have just come out of. I had assumed they'd got rid of him by now. Never did it occur to me that they'd keep him alive this long. But I guess when you have someone you can get information out of, you do what it takes.

"Thank God," Viola says, getting up from her spot on the couch. "Now that he's gone, we can go shopping."

My brows furrow as I look at her like she's the eighth wonder of the world. "You really don't value your life, do you?"

She waves me off. "Please. He doesn't have to know. If he's going to get Vladimir, we'll be back long before he is."

"And what if it's bad intel?" I counter. "What if Vlad isn't there?"

Biting her lip, she considers it for a second. "Then I've heard Cuba is really nice this time of year."

I chuckle and shake my head. "As fun as it would be to watch you get yourself killed, I'm going to pass. I'm exhausted. I really didn't get much sleep last night."

Her hand flies up to her mouth as she fakes a gag. "Please spare me the details of yours and Kage's sex life."

"Why?" I smirk. "You were so keen on knowing them before."

She glances over at me, trying to fight the smile that is forcing its way through. "Bitch."

To be honest, the reason I didn't get much sleep has nothing to do with sex and everything to do with the dreams I've been having. However, there's absolutely no part of me that's going to tell her that. If she wants to believe that Kage and I have been fucking each other's brains out from sun down to sun up, I'm not going to correct her.

"Okay, well, I came all this way," she reasons. "We can at least watch a movie first."

She grabs the remote and switches to Netflix, typing in the movie title. When I see her hit play, I can't help but laugh.

"*Freaky Friday*?" I ask. "Really?"

Shrugging, she grabs one of the throw pillows and makes herself comfortable. "Blame Kage for reminding me about it."

AS THE END OF the movie plays, I keep my eyes closed and my head against the cushion. Faking being asleep became a practiced skill of mine by the time I turned thirteen. It was the only way I could get out of family game night so I could sneak out the fire escape and go gallivanting through the city with Nessa.

I can hear as Viola turns off the TV and slowly gets off the couch, careful not to wake me. The feeling of a blanket being draped over me almost makes me feel bad for not being honest with her, but I need her to leave. She can't be here for what I plan to do.

I listen carefully to the sound of her heels clicking across the tile until the door opens and shuts. Letting out a breath of air, I run into Kage's office and watch the cameras as she gets into her car and drives away.

Finally, I'm alone.

My bare feet pad across the floor as I head for the back door. Stepping outside, the humid, late summer air warms my skin. I quietly shut the door, despite the fact that no one is around to hear me, and cross the patio.

The closer I get, the harder my heart starts to pound. My toes dig into the grass as I cross the yard, until I'm standing in front of the shed. When I see the keyhole on it, I'm almost positive that it's going to be locked. My experiment is going to end before it even begins. But to my surprise, it opens.

Beni must have left in a rush.

I pull the door open and see a man, only a little older than I am, chained to the wall. Dried blood and bruises cover his exposed torso, and his jeans are soaked in what smells like his own piss. The smell is nauseating, but I push down the bile and breathe through my mouth. He lifts his head and sighs in relief when he sees me.

"Oh, thank God," he breathes. "Can you get me out of here? I just want to go home."

I exhale slowly and take a step inside the shed. "Yeah, I won't be doing that."

CHAPTER 9

KAGE

Not only am I not a patient person, but I'm not a trusting one, either. I still haven't fully decided if Viola's intentions with being Saxon's friend are real, or if she's playing some sick and twisted game with someone who's already lost enough. The one thing I do know is that if it ends up being the latter, I won't think twice before taking a machine gun and turning her body into Swiss cheese.

I climb into the helicopter and put the headphones on. Beni does the same and my pilot takes off, bringing the helicopter straight up over my house before heading for the city. I give Beni a look, impatiently waiting for him to explain.

"Right," he says, his voice coming through the headphones. "According to our little *pet*, Vladimir and Dmitri flew back the day after Saxon's funeral. Not many in the organization were aware of it. It was kept pretty low-key, but the shithead has a cousin higher up who told him to put in extra effort because of it."

My brows furrow. "I don't get it. What would make them come back so soon after leaving?"

"A deal," Beni says, making the pieces fall together. "According to him, Dalton is back in, which makes me believe that having Saxon killed was his way of proving his loyalty to Dmitri."

"That wouldn't surprise me in the slightest." A pit settles in my stomach. "Dmitri wanted her dead, because in his mind, she was his property. The second Dalton promised to give her to him, he believed she belonged to him. I didn't tarnish what was *Dalton's*..."

"You ruined what was Dmitri's," Beni finishes for me.

I exhale slowly while pinching the bridge of my nose. "That man is un-fucking-hinged."

"Absolutely delusional," he agrees with me. "But that's neither here nor there. Saxon is safe. Everyone is fully convinced she's dead, and as long as Viola doesn't go blabbing to the media, it will stay that way. In the meantime, we need to focus on *why* they came back to the city."

I shake my head. "It doesn't matter. They put a hit out on Saxon. I'll have them hanging by their intestines off the George Washington Bridge before they can even choose which properties they want first."

Beni nods. "And what about Dalton?"

A sinister smirk makes its way across my face. "I'm going to torture him in ways that make what I've done to everyone else look like a toddler's birthday party."

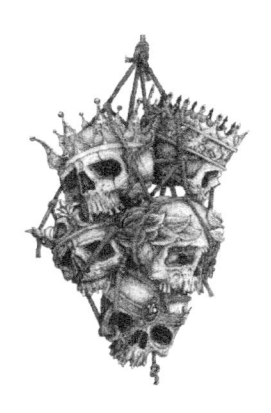

THE RUSSIAN HANGOUT that Vladimir is rumored to be inside sits in the middle of the Bronx. It's a brick building, barren of any windows, with only one way in and one way out. The location could be better, but the building is perfect. It's the ideal place for us to grab him, as long as we can prove he's inside.

Roman and Cesari pull up in a separate car, looking discreet as they make their way past us and into the alley. Beni and I glance around and then follow them, out of view from onlookers. Once we're alone, Ces takes his phone out of his pocket and hands it to me. There, right on the screen, is a picture of Vlad from one of his informants—a crackhead who will do whatever it takes to get the money for his next fix.

My blood starts to rush. The adrenaline of knowing Vladimir is almost within reach has me ready to break down walls with my bare hands in order to get to him.

Another man who stole my father from me will be dying today.

"Okay," I say. "There's not a doubt in my mind that every man in there is armed, so our only option is to go in hot. Thankfully, this isn't the best area, and gunshots aren't uncommon. We kill everyone *except* Vlad. I want him to suffer."

They all nod in unison and turn just in time to see Nico limping as he leads the rest of the soldati behind him. They all look professional, and armed, and ready to take down anyone in their goddamn way. That is, if Ro and Cesari don't take him down first.

Within seconds, two of my most trusted men pull out their guns and have them cocked and pointed at his head. Nico stops in his place, his bruised eyes begging me to rescue him before they blow his fucking brains out.

"You didn't fill them in?" I ask Beni.

He shrugs, feigning innocence. "Must've slipped my mind."

I snort. While the rest of the Familia was at The Pulse for a meeting, where Raff was completely stripped of his *consigliere* title and exiled from the Familia and Nico was beaten by the rest of the soldati for his betrayal, Roman and Cesari were on orders to guard the house. I couldn't risk any of the soldati learning Saxon is still alive. It's already bad enough that Nico knows.

"Lower your weapons," I tell them, finally taking mercy on him. "Beni will fill you in later, but for now we need all hands on deck."

Everyone follows my lead as I walk up to the door, putting one of the newer soldati in front of the peephole. The rest of my men get up against the wall while I knock three times. When a man about my size opens the door, the firefight begins.

I shoot him directly in the head, immediately notifying the rest of the Bratva inside of a threat. My men and I make our way inside with guns blazing, shooting at Vlad's men and taking cover from the returning fire. There are at least twenty men including Vlad, which outnumbers our fifteen, but we're a better shot.

Blood spatters against the walls as we land headshots and take them out one by one, while Vlad remains at the poker table, shuffling cards. He knows there is nowhere for him to go.

A Bratva fires a shot that manages to get one of my soldati in the thigh. He falls to the ground while Nico grabs his arms and drags him to safety. Meanwhile, as another one gets grazed in the arm, he simply uses his other arm to fire his gun right back at them. *That's* the kind of soldati who is going to make it in this organization.

Finally, there's only one gun being fired from the other side, and Beni gets up, running across the room and shooting him directly in the head. The room goes silent, and the only ones left are us and Vladimir. He holds his hands up, careful not to make any sudden moves.

Dead bodies belonging to the Bratva fill the room, and yet we didn't have a single casualty. I step over the bodies, making my way over to Vlad. He glances around with a blasé expression, as if he's not looking at the massacre of his entire team.

"You didn't have to do all that," he says in his thick Russian accent. "I would have gone willingly."

"And ruin all my men's fun?" I mock offense. "I could never."

He's yanked up by Beni and holds his hands behind his back while he gets tied up. "Now that I think about it, it's better that you did. A bunch of pussies like them don't belong in the Bratva."

I snort, watching as Beni grabs his arms and brings them up, making Vlad bend forward uncomfortably. "You're *all* a bunch of pussies."

Roman pulls the car straight up to the door. All my men block the view from the street into the alley while Beni tosses Vlad into the backseat, hogtying him once he's back there.

"We're going to the same place you took Evgeny," I tell Ro. "Meet us there with three soldati of your choosing. Send the rest home."

He nods and takes off to obey my orders. Beni takes the driver's side while I hop in the passenger's side. The SUV peels out of there, making sure we don't have to deal with cops or other Bratva scum who are brave enough to try to rescue their boss.

"Is this really necessary?" Vlad complains, uncomfortable with how he's tied up. "I told you I'd go willingly."

I scoff. "And I'm supposed to believe that bullshit?"

"You should," he says. "I'm tired of running. I've known you were coming for us since the day you took your place as Don. Damn near fourteen years of running and hiding from you is plenty for me."

"Should've killed me when you had the chance," I tell him.

He chuckles dryly. "If I had known you'd grow to have more brain and brawn than your father ever had, trust me, I would've."

I roll my eyes. "Flattery will get you nowhere."

"Fine. Don't believe me. It's no skin off my ass."

WE PULL INTO THE abandoned industrial park and around to the back side of the building. Roman, Cesari, and their chosen few are already waiting, and Nico isn't one of them. *Good*. The last thing I need is him fucking something up. He's been better since I damn near killed him, but this is too important to trust him with.

Ro and Ces come to the SUV and open the backdoor, pulling Vlad out and carrying him by his arms and feet. Beni opens the door and we go inside and down the stairs. The basement is still stained with Evgeny's blood, which is exactly why I wanted to bring Vlad here. I want him to imagine what will happen to him, based on the evidence of what happened to the one before him.

The mental torture is always just as important as the physical kind.

My men put his wrists in the chains that hang from the ceiling, and I grab a metal baseball bat off the table, feeling the weight of it in my hand. I grip the handle and swing it around as I turn to face Vlad. He looks at me like I'm a goddamn amateur.

"Really?" he drawls. "Out of all the weapons you have, you're going to choose a damn baseball bat?"

I smirk. "Yep.

With all my strength, I tightly grip the bat and swing it full force into his knee cap. It shatters on impact as he wails in pain and falls, only to be held up by his wrists. He bites his lip and stands up on the other leg, only for me to deliver the same blow to the next one. With no way to stand, he's left with no choice but to hang there, completely at my mercy.

"I bet you didn't think this would be your fate when you killed my father in cold blood," I sneer. "Right in front of his child, no less."

He takes deep breaths, probably trying to ease the pain and take it like a man, but I'm not having it. I rear back and kick him directly in the center of his chest.

"You fucking answer me when I speak to you."

In his mid-70s, I wouldn't be surprised if a heart attack takes out this man before I do, but the one thing he doesn't get to go with is honor. He may be ready to go, accepting that he's not going to make it out of this room alive. But that doesn't mean I won't make it as brutal and as painful as possible.

"It was the only chance we had," he says. "We tried to take him out for years, and that night, we were out for a few beers and stumbled across the two of you. It was the only time his guard was down."

His explanation is a theory that Raff and I have had for years. My father may not have been a good man, but he was protective of me. Running or trying to fire back would have meant jeopardizing my life, and he wasn't about to do that. So, he took six to the chest.

"For what? You got nothing for his death."

Vlad looks up at me, his eyes narrowed. He's trying to get a read on me, but all I want is answers before I take his miserable ass out of this world.

"No one told you," he concludes.

"Told me what?" I demand. When he doesn't answer right away, I pick up the bat again, this time swinging it directly into his stomach. "Told me what!"

He groans in pain and then coughs as he tries to recover from the blow. "Your father was having an affair with Dmitri's wife."

My whole body goes ice cold. "No."

"For three years, he was fucking her behind your mother and Dmitri's backs," he admits. "When Dmitri found out, he strangled Natalya and tried to kill your father but was unsuccessful. So, he did the only other thing he could to get back at him."

I shake my head, not wanting to hear what's next, because if this is going where I think it is, there is no coming back from it. It will mean that not only did he steal my father from me, but my mother's death was also a result of something Dmitri did.

The fact that my mother was raped was no secret. I was there that night, when multiple men busted in the front door. I still remember the horror in her voice, screaming for me to go hide as she was being thrown to the floor and pinned down.

After that night, she wasn't the same. Some days she wanted to do everything in the world with me, and others, she wouldn't get out of bed. The highs were super high, and the lows were terrifying. And it stayed that way until the day she took her own life, leaving me to find her body.

"*That* was Dmitri?" I growl.

Vlad nods once.

Picking up the metal chair in the middle of the room, I pick it up and throw it at the wall. The sound of it echoes through the room but it's quickly drowned out by me flipping the table. All of the different knives and various weapons scatter, but Roman and Cesari are quick to kick any away from Vlad.

The more the pieces fall into place, the angrier I become, fueling my fire against Dmitri so much more.

He stole my mother's happiness.

He took my father's life.

He tried to have Saxon killed, killing my baby instead.

When I get my hands on that son of a bitch, he's going to experience all the pain the world has to offer. I'll have Antonio keeping him alive, just so I can make sure he gets everything that he deserves.

Beni comes over and puts his hand on my shoulder. I'm about to shove him off, to tell him to let me deal with this. But when I see the look on his face, I know it's serious. He pulls me to the side and shows me his phone—the notification on it sending fear straight through me.

SHED DOOR OPENED. 5:57 PM

"Do you think he escaped?" I ask, thoughts of Saxon immediately flooding my mind.

He shakes his head. "I'm not sure, but the live feed of the cameras doesn't show her anywhere."

I glance at my watch.

6:13 PM.

Fuck!

Turning back to look at Roman and Cesari, I point at Vlad. "Watch him. Make sure he doesn't fucking die."

With that, Beni and I book it up the stairs and out the door. That Bratva shithead isn't in any condition to fight, but if he managed to catch Saxon off guard, there's no telling what he could've done. I never thought I'd say this, but I hope Viola is still there.

DESPITE MAKING THE HALF-hour drive in a matter of fifteen minutes, it's one of the longest drives of my life, coming second to the night Saxon was shot. I jump out of the car before Beni even has it in park and run toward the house —not even stopping to acknowledge the two men guarding the house. The front door is locked, and I fumble to put in the code to open it. When I finally get inside, the whole place is deadly silent.

"Saxon!" I shout.

I'm running through all the rooms I'd usually find her, but she's nowhere to be found. Beni checks the rest of the house, but there's no sign of her there either. We both meet back in the living room.

"Andrea and Giuseppe said they haven't seen anyone," he tells me. "Nothing seemed out of the ordinary."

"Then where the fuck is she?" I growl.

Beni runs a hand through his hair as he glances around, and freezes when he looks into the backyard. "Kage."

Turning my attention to the back door, my heart sinks when I notice the shed door is cracked open.

The two of us sprint full speed out the back door and across the yard, and when I yank open the door, my eyes widen as they take in the scene in front of me. Saxon stands in the middle of the small room, covered from head to toe in blood, but it's not her own. The Bratva rat is behind her, barely clinging to life as cuts and stab wounds cover his entire body. Even one of his ears lies on the floor.

"S?"

I speak softly, like if my tone is too loud, it'll set her off, but she doesn't answer me. It doesn't seem like she realizes I'm here. She just stands there, staring at her own work as if it's the most mesmerizing thing she's ever seen—stuck in a daze.

Carefully, I reach forward and remove the knife from her grasp. After handing it to Beni, I walk around until I'm standing in front of her. Even her face is covered in his blood, and when I put my hands on her cheeks, she finally looks at me.

"Are you okay?"

She blinks up at me—once, twice, three times. And then, to the surprise of Beni and myself, she starts to laugh. It's not her usual giggle though—no. This one is much more sinister.

I pick her up, ignoring the blood that is seeping onto my clothes. As I carry her out of the shed, I stop to speak to Beni.

"Finish him off," I order. "Then get rid of him."

"You've got it, Boss," he answers.

Saxon is practically weightless as I carry her through the house and into the master bathroom. I lock the door behind us and stand her in the middle of the room while I turn on the shower. Once the water is hot enough, I slowly lead her into the shower, our clothes be damned.

The stream rains down on her, rinsing the blood from the top down. She closes her eyes and leans her head back. After a few seconds, her eyes shoot back open and she inhales deeply. Her breathing becomes labored, but not in a way that says she's in trouble. It's in a way that says she's alive.

She grips at my shirt, as if I'm her lifeline. My hand comes up and rests on the wall behind her. I'm towering over her small figure, and when she looks up at me, I know exactly what she needs.

One by one, I strip away each article of her clothing, tossing them into the corner of the shower. Saxon struggles with my shirt, the adrenaline making her hands tremble. In one move, I rip it open and hear the buttons ping as they hit the wall. My cock springs free as I push my pants down and kick them away. I grab Saxon's waist and pick her up, pinning her against the shower wall and slowly lowering her onto me.

Feeling myself inside her again, my balls immediately contract with the need to come. It's everything it always was and so much fucking more. But she needs this more than I do.

Pressing my lips to hers, she moans into my mouth, but I can tell she's holding back.

I break the kiss and pull away just slightly, moving to her ear. "Take it out on me."

And goddamn, she does.

Her nails dig into my back hard enough to draw blood as she pulls me toward her and pushes me away all at the same time. Bringing a hand to my face, she grips my chin and kisses me with such force, I'm sure both our lips will be bruised by the morning.

"Lay on the floor," she demands.

I do as she says, but give her a warning look. "Remember, you're still healing."

She rolls her eyes, straddling me and lowering herself back on my dick. "Treat me like I'm fragile and I'll find someone who won't."

Within a second, I've got my hand wrapped around her throat. "You think what you did out in the shed was brutal? Do that and watch what becomes of *someone*."

The corner of her mouth raises as she gets exactly the reaction she was looking for. Throwing her head back, she starts to ride my dick like she needs it to survive. Her tits bounce, and I reach up to roll her nipples between my fingers.

She grinds down on me, taking every inch of me inside of her, and I can tell she's getting close by the way her eyes fall closed and she digs her nails into my chest. I'm right along with her, climbing higher and higher, getting ready to freefall over the edge, when something dawns on me.

"Sax, you can't let me finish inside you if you don't want to get pregnant again."

Her movements stutter for only a second before she keeps going, quickening her speed. I tightly grip her waist, mindful of her injuries but enough to leave my mark. My jaw locks as she screams out, clenching around my dick while her orgasm explodes.

"Fuck, Saxon!" I growl.

Just before I empty everything I have inside of her, she pulls off and takes me into her mouth. The back of my head presses firmly against the tile floor as I grip her hair and come for the first time in weeks. And she takes every last fucking drop, swallowing it down.

She sits up and licks her lips, and I damn near come all over again.

"You didn't get your vasectomy redone?" she asks as she uses her thumb to wipe away a dab of cum on the corner of her mouth and sucks it off.

I shake my head, my whole body relaxing with relief. "It's not just my decision to make anymore."

And that has her biting her lip to keep from smiling, showing me that the old Saxon is still in there, no matter how volatile this new Saxon may be.

CHAPTER 10

KAGE

VIOLENCE CHANGES PEOPLE. IT SHOWS THEM A different side of things. A side where everything is darker and more dangerous than it's ever been before. And depending on your position, it shows you power. It gives you a taste of what it's like to have someone beg for their life. For that moment, you get to play God, and *that* is what creates a monster.

Ever since finding Saxon in the shed, it's as if something inside her snapped. She's become obsessed with violence and murder, watching crime documentaries like they're the most fascinating thing in the world and making risky moves that she wouldn't have before. And no matter what I do, I can't seem to bring her back from the darkness.

But I'm also not entirely sure I want to.

The depression has changed forms. Before she would lay in bed for hours, sobbing and hyperventilating until she had no energy left to give. But now, she fights. I've found her in the gym more times than I can count, throwing punch after punch into the bag as if it's personally responsible for every bad thing in her life. I have half a mind to bring in Raff and let him train her, but that poses risks I'm not willing to take unless I have to.

All I know is that this version of her is beautifully lethal and terrifyingly dangerous.

"Boss." Roman's voice comes through the phone, snapping me from my dark thoughts. "It's been a week and he's refusing to eat. At this rate, he'll starve to death before you have the chance to kill him."

I run my fingers through my hair and grip tightly. With everything going on with Saxon, I haven't had the ability to get back to causing Vlad's painful demise. My men have been taking care of him in shifts, forcing water down his throat, but there isn't much they can do about food. He'll intentionally choke if he thinks it means dying less miserably.

I'm left with no other option. "I'll call Antonio and have him meet you there."

"I'll have Tomasso keep an eye out for him," he replies.

Hanging up with him, I make a quick phone call to Antonio, telling him to meet me here and I'll give them the location of where I need him. With everything Dmitri has done, I can't chance him finding out where Vlad is being held.

"Give me a couple hours and I'll be there," he tells me.

Having heard all I need to, I end the call and slip it in my pocket. I type up a few emails, making sure my business is still running smoothly. Thankfully, my CFO is someone I met at a conference one year, an Asian man named Elison who would like nothing more than for me to hand the company completely over to him. And as long as he keeps it afloat, I just might.

When I stepped out back to answer the call from Roman, Saxon was sitting on the couch. Now, however, as I come back in, she's nowhere to be found. My pulse quickens as I glance around the room, until the familiar sound of pain meets my ears. I quickly head in the direction of the noise, being led directly to my office.

I exhale in relief as I see Saxon sitting at my desk, but when I realize what she's watching, the dread returns.

For both training purposes and to taunt our enemies, we will sometimes record the violent torture we inflict on others. It's usually a small camera in the corner of the room, and the videos are edited to make sure our faces aren't visible —but the sufferer is fully visible.

Saxon keeps her eyes locked on the screen, watching in amazement. As I make my way over to her, I watch as her hand twitches every time the sound of the knife being stabbed into flesh flows from the speakers. A part of me wants to rip her away from the screen, to tell her that this isn't the life she wants, and that there are other ways to heal. But doing that could push her even further away from me, and I'm just starting to get her back.

"S," I say, getting her attention. "Come have a glass of wine with me."

She nods and gets up from the chair, and I make a mental note to change the password on my computer.

I've been doing everything I can to keep her from becoming a monster like me, but I'm failing miserably. She keeps coming back to it, like a magnet to metal. And I'm not sure how much longer I can shelter her from the violent life of torture and killing.

NEVER IN A MILLION years did I think I would be taking measures to keep Vladimir Mikulov alive, and yet, here we are. The picture that Ro just sent me shows Vlad with his arms and legs tied to a chair. There's an IV in his arm and a feeding tube inserted through his nose.

That'll teach the motherfucker that I will do anything it takes to make sure he dies at my hands and not a moment before I'm ready.

My brain is tired from working all day. I've been spending every free second I have finding everything I can on Dmitri Petrov. Every place he's lived. Every person he has met. Every fucking minute he spends in this city, I want to know about.

It's no surprise that learning what he did to my mother was a shock to my system. I'd always held Dmitri responsible for the devastation in my childhood, but I never knew just how responsible he truly was. And now? I will stop at nothing until I make him suffer through just as much pain as I have.

Getting up from my desk, I stretch my arms over my head and hear as my back cracks in multiple places. I glance out into the living room, having not heard Saxon and Viola in at least a couple of hours, but they're not there. My curiosity gets the better of me, and I venture out to find where they went.

The bedroom is empty, the covers on the bed pulled tight. The jacuzzi on the patio is covered. Even the guest rooms show no sign of them.

I walk into the kitchen, about to call for Beni and send out a search party for them, when I hear the sound of Saxon's giggle coming from downstairs. Relief floods through me only long enough for me to realize there is only one place down there that they would be.

And I locked said place to keep her from drinking herself into liver failure.

Slowly moving down the stairs, I listen as the sound of them gets louder. I turn the corner to see the wine cellar door wide open, and my keys still hanging out of the lock. One of them must have grabbed them from inside my dresser drawer.

It isn't until I make it further inside that my blood pressure starts to rise. There are four empty wine bottles littered across the floor, and the sound of their laughter tells me they're completely wasted. But nothing could prepare me for what I see when I walk around the table.

Everything freezes and time feels like it stands still as I watch Saxon, smiling broadly as she waves a gun around like it's not a deadly fucking weapon.

"Okay, okay." She hiccups. "Ready?"

My heart feels like it stops completely as she puts the gun to her head, and no matter how fast I lunge for her, I can't stop her before she pulls the trigger. The sound of the table being shoved out of the way fills the room and I crash to the floor in front of her.

Every fear I've had over the last month feels like it's playing out in front of me as I scramble to my knees, fully believing I'm going to find her lying dead on the ground, but instead, she's perfectly fine.

Piercing blue eyes stare back at me, blinking as if she can't seem to understand why I practically tackled her. I grab her face and turn her head to inspect for any damage but there is none.

The gun didn't fire.

"What the fuck are you doing?" I bark, finally snapping. "Are you *trying* to get yourself killed?

Her breath hitches, and she doesn't answer. Instead, she tries to look away from me but I'm not having it. I grab her hand, the gun still firmly in her grip, and press the barrel to my chest—straight over my heart.

"Shoot me," I tell her. "If you can kill yourself, you can kill me. It's the same thing. So go ahead. Shoot me."

Her glossy eyes tell me she's intoxicated, but her trembling lip shows that she knows exactly what is happening. She releases the gun, and it falls to the floor between us. I pull her into my arms and suck in air, the first full breath I've taken since I saw her with the gun pressed to her temple. Her head rests against my chest, but it's her lack of emotion that really scares me. With the exception of the one small tear that has escaped from her eye, there's no sign of her feeling anything at all.

"Listen to me," I tell her, pulling her away and forcing her to look at me. "We don't do this. Do you understand me? We don't give in, and we sure as fuck don't give up. We get revenge on our enemies and make them feel the pain of their sins."

Her gaze stays locked with mine as Beni rushes down the stairs, having heard the commotion.

"Everything all right, Boss?"

I don't look away from Sax as I answer. "Yeah. Take Saxon upstairs. I'll be there in a minute."

He comes down and his eyes widen when he sees the empty wine bottles on the floor and the gun in front of me. "Come on, Sax."

She gets up and lets him lead her upstairs, sparing only one glance at me before she's gone.

The moment I'm alone with Viola, I grab the gun and pick her up by her throat, pinning her to the wall. "Are you out of your fucking mind?"

"Kage," she croaks as she tries to pull my hand away.

I let go only to hold her in place by her shoulder and put the gun to her head. "I've almost killed you before. Give me one good fucking reason why I shouldn't do it now."

"I'm not the problem here, asshole. It wasn't my idea, and it's not my gun." She pushes at my chest, but I don't budge.

Where Saxon managed to get ahold of a firearm is the next problem I'll be dealing with, but right now I've got a Familia princess that needs to start explaining herself before his gun becomes lodged in her fucking throat.

"I don't give a fuck whose idea it was," I growl. "Why in the world would you let her play Russian Roulette?"

She puts her hand on the gun and pushes it away from her head. "The gun was empty, jackass."

What? I push the button and move the cylinder so I can check, and sure enough, there's nothing in it. Viola puts one hand on her hip as she glares at me.

"I told you, I'm not the goddamn issue here. And whatever we have to do to fix her needs to be done now, before she plays with someone else and I'm not around to take the bullet out of the fucking chamber." She pulls a single bullet out of her pocket and holds it up before dropping it onto the floor in front of me.

She turns around and marches up the stairs, while I'm left to think about how the hell I'm going to bring Saxon back from the edge.

If I even can.

MY EYES MOVE ACROSS the screen as I scour my resources for anything I can find on who tried to kill Saxon. All last night, I tried to get her to talk to me, but she wouldn't budge. She told me that it's not mine to worry about, which is fucking bullshit. *She* is mine to worry about, and everything pertaining to her goes right along with it. So, if she isn't going to tell me, I'll have to figure it out myself.

Beni taps three times on the door jam. "Boss?"

"What?" I ask, not bothering to look away from my computer.

"Raff is here. Should I let him in?"

My head whips toward him. "What the fuck is he doing here?"

"I'm not sure, but I can ask," he suggests.

"No. I'll find out myself," I tell him. "I have some shit to sort out with him anyway. Let him in but don't let him past the foyer. I'll meet you there in a minute."

Beni nods and leaves my office, heading for the front door. I clean up the papers that are scattered across my desk and collect them into a single pile. Then, with the press of a couple buttons, I lock my computer with its newly changed password.

By the time I get to the foyer, Raff is standing there,

waiting patiently next to Beni with his hands inside his pockets. When he sees me, he gives me that same warm smile he always has, but it doesn't feel like it used to.

"My office," I tell him.

Turning on my heels, I walk back to my office with him following behind. Beni keeps an eye on him to make sure he isn't up to anything, and when we get inside, I shut the door. Anger simmers beneath the surface, primed for the smallest infraction, but I do my best to contain it.

"You shouldn't be here. Your right to just show up unannounced was revoked when you betrayed me and chose blood over the Familia."

He nods. "I know."

My brows raise. "You know, and yet here you are."

"Well, I was hoping I could stop by not as a consigliere, but as the man who helped raise you. Besides, I found something of Silas's I'd like to give to Saxon."

I lean against my desk, resting my hands on the wood and crossing my ankles. "Oh, so you're not here to finally come clean about what a cheat my father really was?" His shoulders sag. "Yeah. Vladimir kindly shared the details about him and Dmitri's wife, and got a front row seat to the angry outburst it caused."

He sighs. "Kage, I wasn't trying to hide things. I just never saw a point in tarnishing your view of him."

"But you did," I argue. "You did keep it from me. And I've spent the last twenty-four years thinking he died an honorable man."

"He *was* honorable," Raff counters. "Don't act like he was running around, fucking any wet pussy he could find. His relationship with your mother was rocky for years before the affair. The only reason they stayed together was *for you*."

"She was *raped* because of his actions!"

"And he beat himself up over that until the day he died!" Raff pauses and takes a deep breath. "Your dad loved you more than he loved anyone, and no matter how many wrongdoings he committed, it doesn't change the fact that he was a good father."

My grip on the edge of my desk tightens. "I'm going to find him."

"Kage."

"I'm going to find him," I repeat. "And when I do, he's going to wish he never so much as spoke of the Malvagio name."

He shakes his head. "You know, I've always said your obsession with avenging his death was unhealthy. You could get yourself killed."

"Then so be it," I answer. "It's not just his death I'm avenging anymore. It's my mother's, and making him pay for the hit he put out on Saxon as well."

"That was Dmitri's doing?"

Pressing my lips into a thin line, I internally chastise myself for saying anything. Raff was outcast from the Familia. That means no longer having a front row seat to information and plans.

"You can give me what you'd like to give Saxon, and then I think it's time you go," I tell him.

He nods and pulls out a pocket watch. It's silver, with the initials S.K. engraved on it, and the chain it's connected to has two charms hanging off of it.

"I had no idea I had it until I was cleaning the other day and found it in the couch," he explains. "He must have lost it at my house the last time he visited."

"I'll make sure she gets it," I assure him.

He thanks me and goes to walk out the door, when he stops and his eyes narrow on the stack of papers on my desk. "What's that?"

I follow his eyes and then shake my head. "You know I can't discuss this with you anymore."

"No," he says. "I know that tattoo."

Picking up the picture—a freeze frame of the video from the moment Paolo was killed—I look it over again. "Where?"

"Right there. On her left wrist." He points to a spot that I assumed was a shadow. "Silas and I took Scarlett to get that tattoo for her twenty-first birthday."

No.

It can't be.

No mother would do that to her child, especially not Scarlett.

I rush around my desk and quickly put in the password to unlock my computer. Opening the video, I let it play and focus on the left wrist. Sure enough, the tattoo is there. I zoom in and play it again, pausing it when she's in a position that makes it most visible.

My eyes narrow as I inspect every inch of the ink, and it all hits me at once, like a ton of bricks.

"You were right about loyalty," Dalton sneers. *"It's a valuable asset, when they're truly loyal to you."*

My mind flashes from that night, to the conversation with the Bratva we had in the shed.

"Ah, you mean Forbes's bitch. The one hanging on his arm all the damn time."

And lastly, Saxon herself.

"Kage, you're not hearing me!" she yells in a panic. "She didn't do it! It wasn't her!"

"How can you be so sure?"

Saxon's shoulders sag. "Because I know who did!"

"Oh my God," I breathe.

I push away from my desk, not caring as the chair crashes into the filing cabinet behind it, and rush out of my office to find Saxon. When I do, she's sitting on the bed, wrapped in a blanket. I walk around until I'm on her side, and kneel down in front of her.

Putting my hands on her cheeks, I stare into her eyes so I know she's listening.

"I get it," I tell her. "Do you hear me? I get it, and you're *not* alone in this. She will pay for what she did to you. They *both* will."

Her eyes start to water. "You know."

I nod. "I know. And I'm on your side. We'll give them everything they've earned. We'll burn the whole damn city to the ground, you and me. If that's what you need, we'll do it. Together."

She throws herself at me, wrapping her arms tightly around my neck while I hold her just as close. I press soft kisses to her shoulder and come to a conclusion that scares me as much as it intrigues me.

"It's time I stop shielding you from the truth."

Chapter 11

Saxon

Heartbreak and betrayal go hand in hand. If you really think about it, there's no having one without the other. After all, betrayal never comes from your enemies. It comes from those closest to you. The ones you were so sure would never do something so cruel.

"Y-you think he killed my grandfather?" I ask.

Kage treads carefully, speaking in soft tones that show me he knows the severity of what he's telling me. "We don't think, babe. We know."

I take a deep breath. Since the day I found out he knew where I was and wasn't so much as trying to negotiate my rescue, I knew my father was not at all the man I thought he was, but this is another level.

"There's more," Kage tells me. "We think she's the one who delivered the final blow, with a dose of air shot into his IV."

That hits me right in the heart. My grandfather was a good man. He had a kind soul and always put his family first. The man would literally give you the shirt off his back if he thought it would make you the slightest bit happier. And for them to do that to him...

"He deserved so much better than that."

Raff nods in agreement. "That he did."

I roll my shoulders back and force myself to stay strong as we keep going. "What else?"

"Sax," Kage says warningly.

"I can handle it," I assure him. "What else?"

He looks like he doesn't believe a single word that just came out of my mouth, but he continues anyway. "Your father was the one who arranged for you to be killed. Your death was required of him to prove to Dmitri that he's trustworthy."

"And then he had the audacity to stand there and look distraught at my funeral," I scoff. "Both of them."

Thinking about it, I get so fired up that I could spit nails. Since the night I was shot, I've grappled with the fact that she was the one to pull the trigger. To fire two bullets into my body and then leaving me there to burn. Hell, at one point, I even started to convince myself that I was delusional. That maybe the pain of being shot was so bad that I imagined the familiar heels stepping over my dying body. But there's no excuse for the truth, and there's definitely no excuse for the betrayal.

"Okay, is that everything, is there something else?"

Kage looks anywhere but at me, his eyes going from one side and then up and around to the other. "For the sake of full disclosure, I killed Brad."

My jaw drops. Out of everything I thought would come out of his mouth, I never thought it would be that. For some reason, him being the reason Brad went missing just never occurred to me.

A giggle bubbles out of me but I swallow it back down. "You killed Brad."

He says nothing, just staring back at me like a deer in the headlights, but I can see the shadow of curiosity. He's wondering how I'll respond.

"Why on earth would you do that?" I ask, but before he can answer, I keep going. "He did nothing to you! Are you *that* twisted that you couldn't stand to see someone else interested in me? I didn't even know your name at that point!"

He grabs my wrist and pulls me into him, making me crash against his chest. "Since you want to know so fucking badly, your *good friend Brad* was trying to slip drugs into your drink so he could get laid. But since we're on the topic, no. I *can't* stand it. I would rather skin myself alive than see someone else's hands on you."

Looking up at him, I don't stand a chance at fighting the smile off that comes from his possessiveness. "You're such a fucking caveman."

AS I LEAVE KAGE'S office, my mind feels like it's on a hamster wheel. So many overwhelming feelings that I don't want to acknowledge threaten to force themselves through. The only thing I can manage to do is force them all down, burying them deep until I'm ready to face them.

Kage would say that I shouldn't do that. That I shouldn't bottle them up like that and should instead take out all my frustrations and daddy issues out on the punching bag. But I can think of something much more effective.

The memory of the guy in the shed is still fresh in my mind, and one I think about often when I need an escape. With every cut and every stab, blood flowed from his body like a river. The way it felt to drive the knife into his stomach is something I'll never forget. And as he screamed, begging for me to stop, I felt stronger than ever.

In there, I wasn't the helpless girl that got kidnapped and held captive, or the girl that got shot and lost her baby.

In there, I was the one who got to decide when he lived and died.

In there, I was the one with all the power.

But instead, I'm here, where the only outlet I have is to cry. And so I do, letting it all out with harsh breathing and clawing at my own chest until it becomes easier to breathe. Kage leans against the doorway, probably feeling as helpless as he looks, knowing that there are times when I need him to hold me and times when I don't. This is one of those times where I just need to be alone in order to feel the pain.

To burn in it.

To live in it.

To survive it.

I WAKE FROM A well-needed nap to find Kage standing beside the bed. He looks conflicted, as if he's not sure about what he's about to do, but he's going to do it anyway. I cock a brow at him, waiting for him to tell me what he wants, when he tosses the same hoodie and hat on the bed that he had me wear when we ended up at Raff's.

"Get up," he tells me. "We're going somewhere."

I sit up and rub my eyes with the back of my hand. "Do I get to know where?"

"No, because I want the ability to turn around if I choose to."

Snorting, I push the blanket off me. "At least you're honest."

I get out of bed and stretch my arms above my head. Kage's eyes move to where my T-shirt rides up, revealing me in a thong. I glance down to see what he's looking at and chuckle.

"Later, babe," I tell him. "Right now you're taking me on a date."

He rolls his eyes. "Considering this a date would make us even more fucked up than I thought."

"Oh, we're definitely fucked up."

I go into the closet and glance at my clothes before realizing I have no idea where we're going.

"What do I wear?" I shout.

He takes a few seconds to answer. "Something you don't mind getting dirty."

That piques my interest and I peek my head out the door. "You're not taking me to dig my own grave, are you?"

"Is that a deal breaker?"

The mischievous smile falls right off my face. "Prick."

Kage laughs and goes into the living room to wait for me. Meanwhile, I pick out a pair of black sweatpants and a matching tank top. I throw on the outfit, paired with a pair of black sneakers, and slip a hair tie onto my wrist just in case. Grabbing the hat and hoodie off the bed, I go find Kage.

When I come out, he looks me up and down, smirking. "Are you dressing to match your soul today?"

"Maybe. You sticking around to find out?"

He looks unsure. "I don't know. You're a bit of a wild one."

My smile widens. "My grandfather didn't call me Wildflower for nothing."

"Whatever you say, Gabbana. Where's your disguise?"

I hold it out to him. "I figured you'd want to do it, being the perfectionist and all."

Chuckling, he starts to put it on me. "Wanting to keep you safe is not perfectionism. It's being protective."

"That's not the word Viola used for it," I say, looking up at him as he puts the hat on me.

"Viola is the bane of my existence."

I tilt my head to the side. "I don't know. I kinda like her."

"I liked it better when you wanted to jab a stiletto into her eyeball," he says seriously. "Can we go back to that?"

"Nope. Now let's go." I grab his hand and start pulling him toward the garage door. "I'm anxious to see where this date is."

"It's not a date."

I tsk. "Nuh-uh. That's for me to decide."

WE END UP TAKING A blacked-out Mercedes Benz, with every window tinted to the point where you can't even see inside through the windshield. The privacy allows me to stare out the window, watching the world pass by as we drive. It's been so long since I was able to just exist that I almost forgot this feeling.

Kage stays quiet for most of the drive, genuinely looking like he might turn around a few times. I glance over at him a few times, and when he can tell I'm getting anxious, he reaches over and covers my hand with his own.

"We're going to where Vladimir Mikulov is being held," he confesses.

I wrack my brain to try to figure out where I've heard that name before. "Do I know who he is?"

"You should. He's one of the men who ordered the hit on you. Dmitri's right hand man, if you will."

"Oh." I turn my attention back out the window. "And why are we going there?"

"To kill him."

His words come out so naturally, like he's talking about the weather or the stocks he bought and sold today, but they catch my attention and hold onto it like Velcro. I whip my head towards him, feeling the adrenaline coursing through me already, and he holds up one finger to keep me from saying anything.

"This isn't what I wanted for you," he points out, "but if it helps you defeat your demons, then fine. But you have to own it. You can't retreat back into yourself when you start to regret the things you've done; guilt is a dangerous bitch, but so is this cold, lifeless corpse that you've become."

I elbow him in the arm, scoffing playfully. "You're lecturing me on feelings? You're so cold that you're completely incapable of love."

"That's not true. I love a lot of things."

"Name three."

He keeps his eyes on the road in front of him as he lists them out. "I love feeling powerful. I love the feeling of my knife as it slides through flesh. I love watching blood pour from my enemies." He looks over at me and smirks in the way that always manages to melt me. "And you."

The breath is sucked straight from my lungs as he turns back to the road as if he didn't just drop the L word while we're on our way to turn someone's insides to minced meat. And he knows exactly what he did as he stares out the windshield with the utmost confidence.

So, I do what I do best, and throw him a curve ball. "That was four. I asked for three."

He glares at me, his amusement evident, and with my tongue pressed against my cheek, I shrug.

Checkmate.

I DON'T KNOW WHAT I expected when Kage told me we were on our way to kill someone, but it definitely wasn't this. He takes my hand and leads me down the stairs of an abandoned building, careful not to let me get hurt.

"There's a rusted part of the stairs right there," he says. "The metal will slice right through your skin."

As we make our way down, I feel my heart start to race.

The bottom of the stairs leads to a dark hallway with only one lit room, all the way at the end. Moisture covers the floor and smells like mold and mildew. The sound of Kage's loafers bounce off the walls with every step he takes.

"You're sure about this?" he asks, stopping outside the room. "Because you can still change your mind. I'll take you home right now."

I bite my lip and nod. "I'm sure."

He presses a kiss to the top of my head before opening the door and walking inside.

An older man is chained to a chair in the middle of the room, his head tipped back awkwardly as he sleeps. Roman and Cesari are both seated on a table, legs dangling, as they mess with their phones. When they look up to see Kage and me, however, they have completely different reactions.

"The fuck is she doing here?" Ces growls, while Ro just smirks.

Kage levels him with a single look. "She does not concern you, Cesari. Make that mistake again, and it might be you in the chair."

Ro holds back a laugh while Cesari goes deadly silent, choosing to watch me with a disgusted look on his face. I have no idea how that man is single, with all of his wonderful qualities.

Kage crosses the room with confidence before grabbing the feeding tube and quite literally ripping it out of his face. "Time to wake up, asshole!"

Vlad startles awake and his arms strain against the chains as he tries to ease the pain, but it's no use. He's trapped. Kage rips out the IV attached to his arm and tosses the pole into the corner of the room.

"It's your lucky day," Kage says sarcastically. "I'm putting an end to your misery. Oh, but not before I make it *so* much worse."

He rolls his eyes, having no patience for any of it. I can imagine he's had enough time to come to terms with the fact that he's going to die. Now there's no panic left. But as he glances over at me and does a double take, there's definitely intrigue.

"Who the fuck are you?"

I smirk as I take a step forward, removing the hat and sweatshirt and tossing them onto a nearby chair. His smile grows as he takes me in until he has his head thrown back in laughter.

"Oh my God," he says, like my being here is the best thing ever. "That's brilliant. Oh, I wish I could be a fly on the wall when Dmitri finds out you're still alive."

Kage lifts one foot and presses it on the cackling man's crotch, adding just enough pressure to make him mewl. "Too bad you won't make it out of this room." He looks over at Roman and Cesari. "Get him up."

As they do what he says, Kage comes over to me. This is the hottest version of him I've seen yet, and the only thing on my mind is what I'm going to do to him after we leave here.

"Still good?" he questions, voice low enough to be for my ears only.

"Never better," I answer honestly.

Vlad screams as they drop him onto his knees before attaching the chains to his wrists and lifting his arms over his head. With a few sharp tugs, they have him hanging from the ceiling, with his feet off the floor.

Kage puts his hand out for me to take and leads me over to the table that's littered with weapons. Everything from knives, to baseball bats, to things I've never seen before. Being most familiar with it, I grab a knife. It's shorter, but the serrated edges look painful.

Walking over to Vlad, he snarls as he looks down at me. "Careful, little girl. Don't want to hurt yourself with that."

I hum, smiling sweetly before jabbing the knife directly into his stomach. The way the blade cuts right through flesh with so little resistance, it's mesmerizing. Vlad roars as blood spews from the wound, but before I can do it again, Kage puts a light touch on my elbow.

"Relax," he tells me calmly. "Killing him is only the inevitable outcome. The goal is to make it as painful and unbearable as physically possible. Take your time."

I look up at him and smile. "Well, in that case..."

Cutting open the shirt that is all but glued to his skin, I press my hands on his ribcage and count the intercostal space. When I find what I'm looking for, I slowly plunge the knife in. It's excruciating, and when his eyes widen, I know I've hit my mark.

"Fucking whore!" Vlad growls.

But Kage isn't about to let that slide. He clenches his fist and decks him right across the face. The sound of his jaw cracking echoes through the room.

"Watch your mouth," he orders. "That's no way to talk to a lady!"

"What did you do to him?" Ro asks.

I smirk, looking up at Vlad. "I just punctured one of his lungs. Nothing fatal."

Walking across the room, I toss the bloody knife onto the table. Now that I know the true objective, I pull my hair up and secure it with the hair tie on my wrist. Kage comes up behind me and puts his hands on my waist. The corners of my mouth raise as I lean back against him, his lips to my ear.

"It should not turn me on this much to see you like this," he murmurs.

I grab the taser and spin around to face him. "Take a seat. I'm just getting started."

Tapping the button while the taser is almost against his chest, it crackles and he steps back. He chuckles slightly as he goes over to stand with Ro and Ces, and lets me do my thing. I inspect the taser as I walk back to Vlad.

"Funny story about these things," I tell him. "They used to scare the shit out of me. I got electrocuted as a kid. You know, the age-old stuck a fork in an electrical socket story. Thankfully, my grandfather was there to grab me before it did serious damage."

"Oh, great," Ces grumbles. "It's fucking show and tell."

I roll my eyes and give Vlad an exasperated look. "Men are always so impatient."

Pressing the taser to his neck, I push the button and watch as his body convulses from the shock. He roars as it flows through him, taking no mercy. When I release it, he's able to breathe for a moment, but just when he thinks it's over, I press it again—this time to his balls.

"Moral of the story is I got over my fear," I yell over the sound of the taser.

As I let go, he lets his head hang and tries to control his breathing—the breathing that is already difficult due to the punctured lung. I go back over to the table and look over all the weapons again. I place the taser down and grab a handle that's attached to a bunch of ropes with metal hooks at the end.

Picking it up, I hold it in my hand and turn toward Kage. "You're into some kinky shit, aren't you?"

He bites his lip as he laughs. "They're cat o' nine tails. You use them like a whip."

My curiosity piques and I look down at the weapon. "Interesting."

I skip back over to Vlad, who still hasn't recovered from the taser. Gripping the handle, I swing it with all my might. The strings whip his body while the metal hooks work as knives, piercing into his skin. Vlad winces at the pain, but when Kage gives me the next instruction, I know it's going to be so much worse.

"Now rip it back out."

I lick my lips and do as he says, watching as each of the metal hooks tear through his skin in the path to their escape. My eyes widen in delight, and I turn back to look at Kage.

"I think these might be my favorite."

Unable to resist, I walk around him, whipping different parts of him and littering his body with cuts. The blood flows over his skin, covering him in a shade of red. Vlad takes it like a man, though. Or at least one with man-flu. He whines like a baby but doesn't try to do anything about it.

Drops of his blood are splattered across my arms and chest, and I'm sure if I wasn't wearing black, you'd be able to see it all over my clothes. And that's exactly how I want it. All the best things in life are a little messy.

Tossing the cattails down onto the table, I grab another blade. A longer one this time, while sticking a smaller one into my back pocket. Vlad has his head tilted back, as if he's waiting for me to just slit his throat and put him out of his misery. Instead, I use him as a dummy, practicing my stab techniques in all the places I know don't have vital organs.

Would you look at that? My pre-med major is useful after all.

I watch in amazement as the knife slides through his flesh like butter and embeds inside him. Everything I've been bottling up lately, all the pain and emotional anguish, it all comes out in the form of torture, and I am more alive than I've been in weeks.

When I'm done, I drop the longer knife and kick it across the floor before pulling the shorter one out of my pocket. Arching up on my tip-toes, I grab the bottom of his eyelids, one by one, and cut slits into them. And as the blood flows out, it looks like he's crying blood.

Finally feeling like I've had my fill, I walk over to the corner where Kage sits between Ro and Cesari. He watches me intently, as he has been the whole time, a look of amazement in his eyes. I put my hands on his chest and move till my lips are against his ear.

"Finish him off," I whisper. "I want to go home, and I want you to fuck me."

He pulls back and smiles, carefully moves me out of the way. "Excuse me."

I hop up onto the table and giggle as Ro puts his fist out for me to bump and then hands me a beer. Taking a sip, I watch in awe as Kage beats and brutalizes Vlad until there isn't a single part of him undamaged. Kage whispers something in his ear and then finally slits his throat so deep it damn near decapitates him.

Pulling a different blade out of his back pocket, he carves the letters A.M. into his torso. Once he's done, he comes over and puts his hand out for me to take. I smile as I hop down off the table and slip my hand in his. He tugs me into him and looks at Roman.

"Brand the words *you're next* under my father's initials and put him right back in the seat at the poker table we took him from," he orders.

Ro nods. "Yes, sir."

Kage drapes his arm over me and leads me from the room. As we get outside, it's dark and pouring rain. My adrenaline is so high that the rain feels ice cold against my skin. I look up at the sky and close my eyes as it washes away all of the pain that's been eating me alive.

I feel Kage's hands on my hips and I spin into him, jumping into his arms and wrapping my legs around his waist. Running my fingers through his hair, I press my lips to his and kiss him like it's the only thing keeping me alive. He smiles against my mouth, and when I pull away, I tilt my head back once more.

It's liberating.

It's invigorating.

It's *everything*.

He puts me down and leads me to the car, opening the door for me before going around to his side. And as he pulls away from the building, I say the one thing that comes to mind.

"Best. Date. Ever."

CHAPTER 12

KAGE

SOME THINGS HAVE A WAY OF MAKING YOU FEEL alive. They reach into your soul and pull at the parts you thought were dead but just needed the right thing to wake them. That's exactly how I felt tonight, and goddamn is it amazing.

I run my fingers through my hair as Saxon sleeps soundly on my chest. It's the first night she hasn't tossed and turned, finally able to get a good night's sleep and not be haunted by nightmares. Her head rests over my heart, and I've never felt more content.

Watching her now, looking so innocent as she sleeps, you'd never believe the little monster she was only hours ago. All I wanted was to keep her away from the violence, but seeing her tonight and the way she inflicted pain on Vlad—she came alive in ways I never imagined.

She may have been born into an elite family and treated like a society princess, but she was destined to be a mafia wife.

With Vladimir taken care of, it's now two down and one

to go—not including Dalton, who Saxon is one-hundred-percent set on killing herself. She says she has a plan for them both, one she intends to keep to herself until the time is right. They deserve to suffer, and there is no doubt in my mind that she will make sure they do.

THE CLOCK IS TICKING, both literally and figuratively, as I stand in front of my house, waiting for Mattia to arrive with one of his friends. Dmitri will have found Vlad's body by now, and knows that we're coming for him next. That's exactly what I wanted, but it comes with its fair share of risks. Dalton is getting closer to having legal possession of all our properties, and the second that happens, he's going to sign them over to the Bratva.

I need to kill Dmitri before that happens.

A black car pulls into the driveway, and the two men get out. Mattia has always been a trusted PI to the family, so when he suggested I hire one of his friends to give him a better chance at finding Dmitri, it was a no-brainer.

"Mr. Malvagio," Mattia greets me. "I'd like to introduce you to Costello Lugeri."

"Nice to meet you," I say, shaking his hand.

He nods. "The pleasure is mine. Mattia speaks very highly of you."

"Yes, well, let's hope he doesn't say too much," I counter.

"Of course," Mattia answers. "So, are we going to go inside and discuss?"

I clasp my hands together. "Unfortunately, I'm having some renovations done. But I have the money here," I pull a stack of bills from my pocket and hand them to Costello. "I added a little extra as an urgency incentive. I'm sure I can trust Mattia to get you up to speed on everything."

Costello's eyes widen when he sees the money. "Oh, okay. You don't have an NDA for me to sign or anything?"

I chuckle, giving him my most charming smile. "Tell you what. You don't fuck me over, and I'll leave your limbs intact."

He swallows harshly. "Understood, sir."

"I thought so." I shake both of their hands once more and nod once. "Thank you, gentlemen. I look forward to hearing from you soon."

With that, I turn around and head back inside. Saxon waits impatiently in the living room, bouncing on her toes while in a tank top and shorts. When she sees me, a smile stretches across her face.

"Are you ready?"

I can't help but snicker at her enthusiasm. "Just let me get changed."

THE HOME GYM I have isn't like many others. While you'd expect to see a bunch of workout equipment, a treadmill, and maybe a bike or an elliptical, that's not the case for mine. Mirrors line two of the walls, making it so you can see the moves you make. The floor is spring-loaded and softer than a usual floor. There's a punching bag in the one corner and different colors of tape sitting on a table with a stereo on it. The only gym-like equipment I have is a set of weights that sit in the far corner by the door, with their own mirror in front of them.

Saxon shifts from one foot to the other as I tape her hands the same way Ralph does mine. Once I'm done, I pick up the focus mitt and hold it in front of me.

"Okay, I want you to punch this as hard as you can," I tell her.

She focuses on it, rearing back and throwing a punch into the padding that I can barely feel.

"No," I deadpan. "Try again. Really throw all your weight into it."

Her eyes narrow, and she tries again, a little harder this time but still not nearly enough. I shake the mitt from my hand and throw it to the ground, stepping toward her.

"Hit me."

She takes a step back. "What? No."

"Come on," I taunt her. "Hit me!"

I take another step toward her, and she takes one more back. "Kage."

"Do it!"

This time she does. She makes a fist and sucker punches me in the stomach, but a quick flex of my abs before impact makes it so she hurts her hand more than she hurts me. I shake my head, wrapping my hand around the back of her neck and pulling her so she stumbles to the other side of the room.

"Take me to the ground, Saxon," I demand. "If you're going to dance with your demons and do the fucked-up things we do, you need to be able to defend yourself. You're not always going to have a weapon to fight someone off with. Take. Me. Down."

Her jaw locks as a look of determination takes over. She moves quickly, dodging my attempt to block her by ducking underneath it. Before I can tell what she's doing, she spins around and kicks backward. Her heel slams into my balls, sending an intense pain straight into my core.

Bile threatens to rise in my throat as I hunch over. Saxon pushes me so I fall to the floor and then climbs on top of me. She smiles sweetly and bends down to press a quick kiss to my lips.

"You said to take you down," she says, shrugging innocently.

I cough as I both laugh and catch my breath. "That's twice now. Keep it up and we won't be able to have kids, vasectomy re-do or not."

Her nose scrunches up as she sticks her tongue out at me, until the sound of someone clapping catches both of our attention. Both our heads turn to see Ralph standing in the doorway.

"I have to admit, I'm impressed," he says. "I wish I knew the rules. Your winning streak would be much shorter."

Saxon climbs off of me and stands up while Ralph extends his hand to me. As I take it, he pulls me to my feet. S looks confused as she looks between the two of us.

"Ralph, this is the woman I told you about."

He turns to face her and puts his hand out. "You look great for being a corpse."

"Thank you. You look like you're ready to become one yourself," she quips, poking fun at his age.

A deep belly laugh rolls out of him. "Now I see how you're able to hold your own with this one. I may look old, but I'll have you know I'm in the best shape of my life."

"The activities at the senior center will do that for you."

He chuckles some more and turns to me. "I like her."

"I thought you would," I reply. "You're actually going to be training *her* this week."

"Is that so?"

I nod, giving Saxon a reassuring smile. "In my line of work, I can't have her unable to defend herself. As you saw, she's resourceful, but she's no match for some of my enemies. I just happened to trust her a little too much. Let my guard down."

She rolls her eyes, and I nudge her with my elbow as Ralph smiles.

"Well, it looks like I have my work cut out for me then."

"That you do. I'll be back in a bit, but Beni will be here if you need anything."

I give Saxon a quick kiss before leaving them alone.

Letting Ralph in on the secret that Saxon is still alive isn't a decision I took lightly. And that's not because I don't trust him. It's simply because the more people that know about her resurrection, the riskier it is. But the pros outweighed the cons in this scenario. Knowing how to fight is important, and if she plans on staying in this life with me, doing what we do, it's absolutely vital.

Beni is sitting in my office, going through some of the information that Mattia and Costello sent this morning. There's everything from old security footage from local spots in the city to credit card statements from hotels. How he manages to get ahold of this stuff so quickly is one of the reasons why he's paid so well.

"I'm heading into the city," I tell him. "Stay here with Saxon and call me if anything comes up."

"You've got it, Boss."

I go into the bedroom to change back into my suit and then head out the door. The pilot, a reputable man named Jensen, holds the door open for me, and I climb into my helicopter. He walks around and gets into his seat, clicking all the appropriate buttons and speaking into the radio for take-off.

"Ready to go, sir?" he asks.

I nod. "Whenever you are."

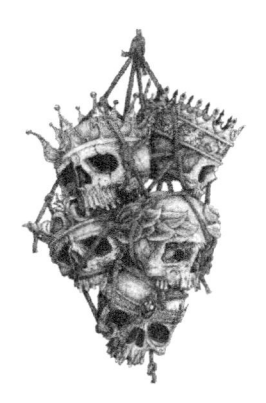

STAYING DISCREET HAS NEVER been my style. I've always liked being in the front lines of it all and not hiding in the background. It's one of the reasons people fear me. What kind of psycho has enough people working for him to delegate every single thing in his life but still gets his hands dirty?

This one.

But this time, staying hidden is exactly what I need to do. If they catch me watching, everything will unravel, and we'll lose our chance at getting revenge for Saxon. And I don't want to see what she's like if she's unable to make them pay for what they did to her.

I keep my head low but my eyes focused in front of me as I watch the two of them come out of Dalton's office building. They're all smiles, as if they haven't lost one of the most important people in their lives. They look like they're on top of the world, when they should be counting their days.

They get into the car, and as it pulls away from the curb, I wait for a few cars to pass before following behind. It's both easier and harder to tail someone in New York City. The traffic makes it harder for them to spot you, but it also becomes much easier to lose them. To successfully follow someone, you need to have practice and skill.

Reaching their destination, I watch as she gets out of the car and runs into Elite Gym. A few moments later, she comes out, swinging Kylie's hand and tickling her as she lifts her into the car. My heart hurts for the little girl. She's going to mourn the loss that is coming to her, but she has no idea what her older sister is saving her from.

I end up following them all the way to the restaurant they're having dinner at, and as the three of them walk inside and take their seats, I've seen enough. Any more and I'll end up going in there just to slit their throats myself. Having eyes on them reminds me why I'm standing by and watching Saxon become what she is.

A gorgeously lethal, cold-blooded killer.

GETTING BACK TO MY house, I go straight to the gym and find Saxon and Ralph both covered in sweat. He's got his hands on his knees, panting, while Saxon is lying on the floor like a starfish. I cock a brow at them and smirk.

"When you said you have your work cut out for you, I didn't think you meant you were going to do it all today," I joke.

If I'm honest, I thought he would be long gone by the time I got back.

Ralph waves me off dismissively, while Saxon giggles. "He's just mad because I already beat him four times on my first day."

I can't help the prideful smile that stretches across my face. "That's my girl."

"Your girl is downright homicidal," Ralph growls between pants.

Trust me, I know.

"Take the day off tomorrow," I tell him. "I have other plans. We'll see you Wednesday afternoon."

He nods. "Probably for the better. I'm bound to be sore after that workout."

Saxon sits up and smiles sweetly at him. "So much for being in the best shape of your life."

Ralph still finds the energy to laugh. "Kage was right. You really are a menace."

"I warned you," I say, and Saxon blushes as I wink at her.

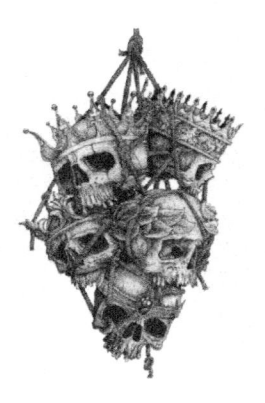

THE NEXT DAY IS a terrifying one, given her track record with revolvers, but a necessary one all the same. Pulling around to the back of the building, I park between two dumpsters and climb out of the car. After I grab the bag from the trunk, Saxon follows me to the door, looking around as if we're doing something wrong.

"Is this place even open?" she asks. "Why aren't we going in through the front door?"

I ignore her questions and stick the key in the lock. As soon as I open the door, the alarm starts to beep. It gives me a total of thirty seconds to disarm it, but Saxon only gives me two before she freaks out.

"Oh, great. Now the cops are going to come," she frets. "How are we going to explain to them that a dead girl can't sit in county?"

I focus on putting in the code, silencing the alarm. When I finally turn my attention to where she's standing, she presses her lips into a thin line and tries to pretend like she doesn't have foot-in-mouth syndrome right now.

"Anything else you'd like to comment on?"

She shakes her head. "Nope."

"Good," I answer. "For your information, I own this place."

Looking around, as we walk toward the front of the building, she hums. "And *this place* is what exactly?"

I place the bag on the counter and pull out the revolver she used to shoot at me. "A shooting range."

She gasps, grabbing it from me. "Oh, Jack! I thought the old lady dropped this in the ocean at the end."

Staring back at her, I shake my head. "I am *not* quoting Britney Spears with you. You have Viola for that."

A mischievous glint sparkles in her eyes. "Do you want to talk about how you instantly knew where that was from?"

I go to walk away from her, and she breaks out into a horrible rendition of "Oops…I Did It Again" while following behind me. Walking through the doors and down the few sets of stairs to the stalls, I take the few guns I brought with us and put them on the different counters. When I'm done, I turn and put my hand over Saxon's mouth.

"Remind me to get you singing lessons as well if you're going to do that."

She starts to pout and then changes course, licking my palm. My brows furrow as I watch her look surprised when I don't get grossed out.

"Your pussy was literally on my face last night," I point out. "You really think your saliva is going to bother me?"

Saxon rolls her eyes and smacks my hand away from her face. "Okay, so what are we doing here? Is this where you kill me and bury me next to wherever you put Brad?"

I turn and go to the first stall. "If I was, you're not making a very good argument for keeping you alive."

"I give good blowjobs," she says, catching me off guard.

Laughter bubbles out of me. "That's true. You give

phenomenal head, but maybe stick to using your mouth for just that."

Her jaw drops as she mocks offense. "Maybe you should be more mindful before you go insulting the girl holding a gun."

"You've tried firing that thing at me before," I tell her as I hang the target. "It didn't go well for you then, and I can assure you it wouldn't go any better now."

With a snicker and a quick mimic of my words in a higher pitched tone, our banter comes to an end. Little does she know, I secretly love when she's like this. It's in these times that the old her shines through and reminds me she's still there. Not that I'm not crazy about this new, volatile version of Saxon. It's just that I'm a greedy son of a bitch when it comes to her.

I want them all.

"Okay, come here," I tell her, and she does, moving to stand in front of me.

I put a pair of sound mufflers and safety glasses on each of us. With her hands holding the gun, I take them in mine and help her raise them up, aiming the revolver at the target. Her hand trembles slightly, but as I press my lips to her shoulder and whisper for her to breathe, she calms.

"When you feel like you're ready, aim for the target and shoot until the gun is empty," I instruct her.

She does what I say, and after a few seconds, the sound of gunshots fills the room. I count to six in my head and on seven, she goes to pull the trigger, but nothing comes out. She puts the gun down on the counter and smiles back at me. However, when I press the button to bring the target back, the smile falls right off her face.

Out of all six shots, she managed to land two.

"Okay, so maybe my aim could use a little improvement," she says, as if she was only a little off.

In actuality, the ones she managed to shoot through the

paper aren't even on the actual target. One is above his head, while the other is in the bottom right corner.

This is going to be a long day.

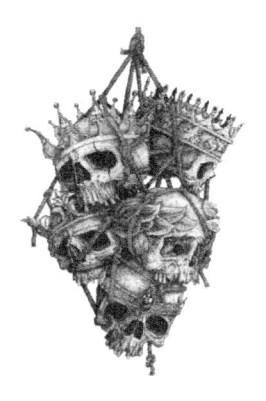

THEY SAY THAT PRACTICE makes perfect, and I'm sure that's true. However, I'm thinking Saxon with a gun may be the exception. She shot for four hours, going through all the bullets I brought with us and every single gun. Well, other than the machine gun. There are just some guns that are too big for little girls.

Out of all of it, she only got to be as good as Nico, and that's not saying very much. I've watched that idiot shoot a gun and manage to outline the target. And trust me when I tell you that it was *not* intentional.

"When are we going back?" she asks excitedly.

I wince at the question. "I don't know. I'm starting to think you're better with other toys. Like the cat o' nine tails. They can be your signature—like the happy face killer."

She rolls her eyes and plops down onto the couch. "Fine. I'll just get Beni to teach me."

Now *that* isn't the worst idea. That man is a better shot than I am.

I go into my office and over to my half-ton safe. I place my hand on the reader and then turn the five-spoke handle to open the door. One thing I've always taken very seriously is putting all the guns away after the range. Other than the one that stays on me for protection purposes, it's important they stay locked up. The last thing I need is for these to end up in someone else's hands.

I'm putting them all back in their rightful places when the light reflects off a picture frame on the top shelf and catches my attention. I drop the bag beside me, taking out the frame, and seeing the familiar picture inside of it.

I'm nine years old, standing in front of my parents with the biggest smile on my face. My dad's arm is around my mom, and they're both posing happily for the picture, but now that I know the background behind it, it doesn't feel the same.

It used to gut me. I can't remember how long this picture sat on my desk as I searched for the three men who killed him and came up empty. Finally, I had to accept the fact that it wasn't healthy anymore and needed to put it away. I just forgot that I put it in the safe.

Knowing this picture was only about a year before my mom killed herself, I now know that while they looked happy, it was a sham. The reality is that my father was fucking the enemy's wife while his own was at home, raising their son.

I've spent the last couple weeks pushing it down and ignoring it, still carrying out the plan of avenging his death just as ardently as ever. But standing here, staring at this picture, I can feel it all come racing to the surface. Because the truth is I'm still angry and with every fucking right to be. Everything I thought to be true about my father being an honest and noble man was a lie.

He was a liar and a cheat, and he had just as much of a hand in my mom's suicide as Dmitri did.

My grip on the frame tightens as my blood starts to boil,

and when I can't contain it anymore, I throw it across my office. It hits the wall and shatters into a thousand tiny pieces, with the photo inside floating gently to the ground. And I know it's only a matter of seconds before Saxon comes in and makes me face it, like I've done with her.

"Kage?"

Chapter 13

Saxon

Strength is never something I thought was important for me. I was a trust-fund brat whose only focus was moving out of my parents' penthouse and living on my own. And since the rule was that I couldn't live alone until I graduated from college, that's what I spent all my energy on.

But then Kage happened, and everything that came along with it. And being strong became the only thing that kept me alive. That helped me live through one day and to the next. I may have faltered, but I pushed through. And now, as a dead girl, I feel more alive than I ever did as the billionaire's daughter.

I'm sitting on the couch, flexing my finger and wincing at how sore it is from constantly pulling a trigger over and over, when the sound of something breaking comes from Kage's office. Beni and I both get up and rush in there to make sure he's all right, but when we see the family photo on the ground surrounded by pieces of glass, I put my hand on Beni's shoulder.

"I've got this."

He nods and goes back to whatever he was doing, while I step inside the office, careful not to step on my glass.

"Kage?"

He looks over at me, and when he sees me in the middle of the mess, his eyes widen. He comes over and picks me up by my waist, lifting me over all the shards. When he puts me down, I rest my hands against his chest and look up at him.

"Are you okay?" I ask.

He forces a smile, but it doesn't reach his eyes. "I'm fine. I just missed the garbage can."

I hum and point to the total opposite corner of the room. "You mean the one that's over there?"

He looks toward where I'm pointing and sighs.

Carefully, and much to his dismay, I go over to the photo and pick it up. It's definitely older, taken with film and developed rather than printed like we do these days. A smaller, younger version of Kage stands front and center at the beach, dressed in a Teenage Mutant Ninja Turtles shirt and a grin from ear to ear. Behind him are a beautiful couple. The man is dressed in a black suit like Kage wears, with his hair slicked back and a pair of very familiar eyes, while the woman beside him is wearing a light-colored dress.

It looks like they just came from a dinner, and I can tell why Kage would hold onto such a photo. What I can't understand is why it was able to take his mood from one-hundred to zero and why the frame is in pieces.

"Do you still have that T-shirt?" I joke, lightening the mood. "It's definitely your style. You should wear it more often."

He huffs playfully and snatches the picture out of my hands. "I'll have you know that TMNT was all the rage when I was a kid."

"You mean in days of yore?"

The glare he gives me is one that tells me he's trying to be in a good mood, but it's slipping. I walk over and tuck myself into his side, feeling content as he wraps his arm around me and the two of us look at the picture.

"I can see where you get it from," I tell him.

He looks down at me. "What?"

"Your looks. You've got your mom's beauty with your dad's ability to look intimidating while smiling."

As if he hadn't noticed it before, he squints as he looks at the picture once more. When he's done, he exhales slowly and puts the photo in his safe.

"Too bad he was a fucking liar," he mutters.

My brows furrow. "Your dad?"

"Yep. The day we took Vlad, he generously filled me in on the fact that my dad was fucking someone else behind my mom's back." He goes quiet for a minute and then scoffs. "Dmitri's fucking wife, of all people."

I feel his pain, maybe more than he realizes. Finding out that your father isn't the person you spent your whole life thinking he was is a hard pill to swallow. It makes you question everything else around you, because if something you were so sure about turned out to be a lie, how can you be confident in everything else in your life?

"I get it," I tell him. "That's really shitty of him."

"You don't even know the half of it," he says, shaking his head.

I shrug. "I don't, but I'm here to listen if you want to tell me."

His gaze locks with my own, and for a minute, we just stand there, until the smallest hint of a smile peeks through. He breaks our eye contact and holds me close, rubbing the skin of my hip with his thumb.

"His actions were what kicked everything in motion," he confesses. "Because of what my father did, Dmitri and some of his goons raped my mother. And because of the rape, my mother spent a year spiraling out of control before she finally committed suicide. Then when Dmitri finally got the chance, he killed him." He pauses to think for a moment. "I just can't help but wonder—if he had kept his dick in his pants, would my entire life have been different? Would they still be here right now, having family game night at Raff's and lecturing me on how I should be running things?"

I take a deep breath, letting everything he said sink in. "I think playing *what if* is a very dangerous game. One that has no winner. And with the world you live in, there's no guarantee he wouldn't have been killed anyway. That may sound harsh…"

"But it's the truth," he says. "Pissing people off *was* his specialty."

Giving him a small smile, I rest my head on his chest. "All I'm saying is I don't think you should let someone like Vlad and Dmitri ruin the memory you have of your father. Take it from someone who has the shittiest one of them all."

He snorts, pressing a kiss to my hair. "Yours really is the worst."

"Exactly, and allowing them to make you think your father is comparable to mine is letting them win, and that's beneath you. Don't give them that power."

I grab his hand and lead him out of the office. While I tiptoe around the glass, Kage uncaringly steps right through it. As we pass by Beni sitting on the couch, I lean over the back of it.

"Would you maybe mind cleaning up the mess in Kage's office?" I ask sweetly.

He smiles and turns to look at me. "You mean, you aren't going to try slitting your wrist with the glass this time, Kamikaze?"

Taking my hand, I smack him lightly across the back of the head. "Not this time. But I'll give you the heads-up if I ever plan on doing that again. Get you a front row seat this time."

As he gets off the couch, he chuckles. "I appreciate it."

Kage and I go into the bedroom and shut the door behind us, and before I can even reach the bed, he grabs my wrist and pulls me back into him. His gaze is intimidating as he stares down at me, but he softens when I reach up and kiss him.

"If you ever cheat on me, I'll kill us all," he warns. "You, the guy you're fucking, and myself. I'll make your antics look like a skinned knee."

I giggle, knowing he's telling the truth but also knowing he never has to worry about that. "You always say the sweetest things."

"Saxon."

Sighing, I put my hands on his face. "That will never happen. Not in this lifetime, and not even in the next."

"Good," he says, content with that answer. "Just know that if you do…"

"I won't."

And I mean that more than I've ever meant anything.

ONE OF MY FAVORITE things about Viola is her ability to make Kage go from laughing to an angry shade of red in record time. She throws her hands in the air as she once again isn't getting the answer she wants from him, and he glares at me, as if silently saying *this is your friend, you deal with*

her. I, however, am completely content with sitting here and watching this comedy show unfold.

"Okay, can you take the stick out of your ass for all of five seconds and let me talk?" she argues.

He stares back at her, emotionless. "Not if you're going to give me more reasons why you think it's a good idea for Saxon to leave the house, no."

She throws her arms in the air. "Oh come on. She's been cooped up in the house—with the exception of your little murder party—which, don't even get me started on that…"

Kage and I both laugh as he glances over at me. "That's not true. I took her to the shooting range, too."

Viola's head falls back. "Ugh! Your relationship is doomed to fail if you think she's not going to lose her absolute mind being stuck in here with you all the time. I could barely do it when we lived together."

"False," he claps back. "You were in love with me when I lived with you."

She freezes then scrunches her nose like she forgot that was even a thing. "We don't talk about that."

"Agreed," I chime in.

Viola looks at me like she finally remembers I'm in the room. "S, please. Tell him you need to get out of this place and see the world."

Kage looks at me with brows raised as I purse my lips. "I mean… It has been months since I was able to go shopping."

Viola shouts triumphantly while Kage's jaw drops as he glares at me. "Traitor."

I bring my energy drink to my mouth and sip through the straw, looking around the room innocently. Knowing she has my back, Viola redoubles her efforts and picks at Kage until his already short patience is close to eviscerated.

"Ah-ha!" She snaps her fingers. "I have an idea, and it is *brilliant.*"

"That's new," Kage drawls, but she ignores him.

Viola's eyes meet mine and she looks me up and down, like she's sizing me up. "How confident are you in your fighting skills?"

Kage looks around, as if she's personally threatening him, and I chuckle as he waits, concerned about where this is going.

"I mean, I've been training with Ralph for about a week now, and I think I've gotten pretty decent," I answer. "Why?"

A conniving smile appears on her face and she turns to Kage, crossing her arms over her chest. "The two of you spar. If you win, we don't go. But if Saxon wins, we get to go shopping."

"Not a chance in hell," he says before she's even done talking.

"Why not?" she teases. "Afraid you're going to get your ass kicked by your own woman?"

He points at me while keeping his eyes on Viola. "She doesn't fight fair, and my balls can't take much more."

I cover my mouth, giggling into the sleeve of my sweatshirt. "Oops?"

"Yeah, oops," he grumbles.

Viola sighs. "Okay, so we set ground rules. Restricted no-no area for her, and you can't lift her up off the ground."

I'm not going to lie; it's a good deal. One that Kage knows if he turns down, Viola will never let him live it down. She'll forever harp on him about that one time he was too afraid to go up against a girl. And I think he knows that, because he leans forward with his elbows resting on his knees and turns his head toward me.

I wink at him and blow him a kiss, taunting him, and somehow it works. He rolls his eyes and sighs before standing up.

"Fuck it," he murmurs. "Come on, Gabbana."

"Yes!" Viola cheers.

Kage flicks her in the forehead. "Don't get ahead of yourself. She has to beat me for you to win."

"Are you kidding?" she snaps back. "I'm confident in my girl. We'll be at the mall before sundown."

Suddenly, he looks like he regrets his decision as he drops his head and starts walking toward the gym. I climb off the couch and follow behind. Viola waits for me and clings to my arm the second I'm close enough.

"Okay, so I'm thinking fuck the rules," she whispers. "Go for the balls and while he recovers, we'll book it out of here."

I can't help but laugh. "That sounds like it came straight from the manual on how to get yourself killed by a mafia don."

She shakes her head. "Nonsense. He doesn't have it in him to kill you."

"It's not *me* I'm worried about."

The three of us get into the gym, and Kage seems so ready to get this over with that I'm almost afraid of how fast I'm going to lose. I stand across from him, the two of us taunting each other with our eyes. Viola puts her hand in between us and recites the terms.

"First one to get their opponent on their back wins," she says. "And remember, Malvagio, no funny business."

He snorts. "Yeah, because I'm the one here who fights dirty."

"Go!"

We spin in circles, both of us holding up our hands and ready to swing. Knowing he won't actually hit me, it gives me a little bit of an advantage as I throw punches in his direction. But each one, he manages to dodge.

The longer we go, the longer I realize I don't stand a chance at beating him. The first time, when I took him to the ground in under ten seconds, was beginner's luck. He was taking it easy on me. But this time, he has a stake in it. If he loses, it doesn't just mean I win—it means Viola does, too.

My mind wanders to the days I used to spend shopping all afternoon. I'd swipe my credit card until the strip was damn near worn off, and then I'd go home and try it all on, thinking about how I didn't get enough. It was my one guilty pleasure —one I haven't been able to indulge in since Beni all but snatched me from *The Pulse*.

I want this.

I fucking need it.

"Wait," I say, stopping. "I have to pee."

Kage straightens his back and looks at me in disbelief. "Seriously? Now?"

"Nope."

Before he sees it coming, I swoop my leg behind his and throw the upper half of me at him, sending both of us to the ground. Kage puts his hands on my waist to keep me safe while he slams against the floor. And the next thing I know, Viola is jumping up and down, screaming and cheering.

"We get to go shopping!" she singsongs.

I climb off of Kage and bite my lip to contain my smile as he glares back at me. "Once a cheater, always a cheater."

"If it works on you, it'll work on anyone."

He sits up and leans back against his hands. "Okay, fine. But can I make some conditions, for the sake of her safety?"

Viola stops cheering and rolls her eyes. "What now, buzzkill? And it better not be wearing that sad excuse for a disguise. She's not looking homeless. The stores won't even let her in."

Ignoring her, he keeps his eyes on me. "We go tomorrow. I'll get someone to bring us a professional quality wig and colored contacts. Viola will do your makeup, and the *three* of us will leave in the morning and go to Rhode Island, where there is a much lower chance of you being recognized."

It's not an unreasonable counteroffer. Everything he's suggesting *is* in my best interest, and we can make a day of it.

I glance over at Viola, surprised to see she's actually willing to compromise.

"Okay," I agree. "You've got yourself a deal."

He smiles that killer smile that always manages to trip me up, and he grabs my wrist to pull me down. I straddle his waist and wrap my arms around his neck, kissing him deeply. His hand moves to the back of my neck to pull me impossibly closer. I'm so lost in the feeling of him, I barely notice as Viola gags and walks out of the room.

"You scared her off," I murmur against his lips.

Kage smiles into the kiss. "Good. That was part of my plan."

TRUE TO HIS WORD, the next morning—after a makeshift transformation that turns me into a brunette with green eyes—we hop in the Escalade to head to Rhode Island. Viola follows behind in her Ferrari, wanting to drop it off at her place before we go. Kage reaches over and laces his fingers with mine.

"I still don't like this," he says.

I squeeze his hand. "I know, but you like me."

"Something like that."

It doesn't take long before we're pulling up to Raff's, where Viola is staying, and she pulls into the driveway before making an excuse to run inside for a moment. Raff comes out and walks over to the driver's side of the car, and things seem better between the two men than they have been lately.

"Vi said you're all taking a road trip?" he asks.

Kage groans. "Her and this one becoming friends is going to be the death of me."

Raff chuckles and looks over at me. "Sending him to an early grave, are you?"

"Mr. Dramatic will be just fine," I say with a smile.

"After we get back, I want to sit down with you," Kage tells him. "Bury the hatchet and all that."

A genuine smile appears on his face. "I'd like that, son."

Viola comes walking back out from the house with Nico in tow, and I can practically feel Kage's mood shift. The two of them bounce down the steps, and Viola smiles cheerfully as she opens the back door.

"Little brother is coming with," she says.

Kage shoots a look my direction, silently telling me that this is partly my fault. "Fucking splendid."

Nico gets into the car behind Viola. "Vi, we're twins. We share a birthday."

"Yes, and I was born before you, which makes you *little brother*," she reasons.

Thankfully, he lets her win this one and puts his hand on my shoulder. "Hey, S. You look good."

I smile back at him while Kage glares hard into the rearview mirror. Nico refuses to make eye contact, instead choosing to stay focused on me.

"He's killing me in his mind, isn't he?" he questions.

"Check her out one more time, and it'll be a lot more than in my mind," Kage threatens.

Nico settles back into the seat. "That's fair."

THE DRIVE TO RHODE Island isn't the longest one I've ever taken, but with the Mancini twins in the car, it feels like a whole decade. The amount of times those two go from being the best of friends to arguing is enough to make your damn head spin. And by the time Kage parks the car in the middle of a small shopping strip downtown, he and I are damn near lunging to get out.

"This place is cute!" Vi says as she looks up and down the street. "But where are the designers? Or even Nordstrom or Bergdorf. Where did you bring us?"

Kage drapes his arm over my shoulders. "Somewhere *safe* where you can still shop."

She cringes as she looks in the window of the thrift store in front of us. "Great. So, if she dies, it'll be styleless."

Nico spots a bar across the street and taps Kage's arm with the back of his hand. "What do you say we go grab a beer while the girls shop?"

Kage isn't having it. "If you think I'm taking my eyes off her for a second while we're here, you're out of your goddamn mind."

"No beer it is then," Nico agrees.

WE MANAGE TO FIND a few cute boutiques that may not be name brand, but they are unique. The one-of-a-kind appeal they have changes Viola's opinion of this place, and she finally starts having fun.

The four of us find a cute little restaurant by the beach to have lunch, and I can't deny how good this feels, to be out in the open, without feeling like I have to constantly look over my shoulder. Granted, Kage is doing that for me, but he's constantly on edge when it comes to me. Not that I can say I blame him. He did watch me almost die...twice.

"You okay?" he asks, noticing me staring off into space.

I smile back at him and nod. "I like it here. It's small and feels like it's in the middle of nowhere, but it feels easy."

He reaches under the table and grabs my hand. "It's definitely less chaotic."

As Kage takes a sip of his beer, I go back to looking around again. I could see myself settling down in a place like this, off the grid, where your every move isn't being documented simply because of who you're related to. This feels like my kind of place, and I find myself wondering if Kage would ever leave New York.

BEFORE DECIDING TO HEAD back, Viola and I convince Kage to hit one more strip, mainly for the bakery. He looks entirely fed up with our shit but ultimately agrees. It takes twenty minutes to get there with traffic, but when I see all the different cupcakes they have, I declare it worth it.

We're walking down the street, licking the icing off our dessert, when my eyes land on a tattoo parlor. An open sign hangs in the window with the name of the place in graffiti style artwork above it.

Get Inked.

"Can we stop in here?" I ask, already heading for the door.

Kage's eyes narrow. "If you wanted a tattoo, you could've told me. I have an artist."

"In *New York*, where they're not allowed to know I'm alive," I counter.

He reaches forward and grabs the handle, opening it for me. "After you."

We all enter the tattoo shop, and I look around at the artwork that papers the walls. A guy around my age gets up from his seat. His black hair swoops to the side, and the band T-shirt he's wearing allows me to see that his arms are covered in tattoos.

"What can I do for you guys?" he greets us.

I snatch Viola's phone out of her hand and type in what I'm looking for. When I find it, I turn the device toward him.

"I want this on my back."

He picks up the phone, zooming in on certain details of the tattoo. "This is a pretty big piece. You're looking at being here all night for something like that. I was planning on heading out, but if you want to do it tonight, I'll stay."

I look up at Kage, knowing that he wants to hit the road, but also not knowing when the next chance I'll get is. As he looks back at me, I smile sweetly until he finally caves, waving his hand as if to say *go ahead*.

"Sounds good to me," I tell the tattoo artist.

"Great," he answers. "I'll get this drawn up…"

"Viola," I fill in for him, making Vi choke on air.

He nods. "Sweet. I'm Knox. And these are?"

Nico introduces himself first, being the second most social, but Viola is clearly scrambling to think of a fake name. Kage is busy sizing Knox up but manages to grumble out his name. When Knox turns to Viola, she looks like a deer in the headlights.

"Kanicola," she blurts.

My jaw drops as I admire her absolute stupidity, while Knox looks at her like he's wondering if she's okay.

"Y-you want a can of cola?"

It takes everything I have not to break into hysterics.

"I'm sorry. She's a little slow," I tell Knox and turn to Viola. "Your name, sweetie. He wants to know your name."

"I'm Ellis," she practically shouts, and my God her lying needs work.

Out of all the names she could have picked, and she picks one that sounds like we snatched her from the closest nursing home. Even Knox has to hold back from laughing as he takes the phone into the other room.

"Give me a minute to get a stencil made and I'll be right back," he says.

I nod and he disappears, pulling out his own phone before he walks through the door.

Turning to Viola, I break into hysterical laughter. "Way to go, *Ellis*. And Kanicola? What the hell was that?"

"Fuck you. My brain mixed the three names together." she grumbles. "And you're the one that stole my name, you bitch."

"Well, I couldn't exactly use my own."

She rolls her eyes and flips me off as I'm still chuckling at her name choice. Even Nico whispers something about calling her that from now on, though if the threat she throws back at him holds any weight, I doubt he'll actually do it.

A few minutes later, Knox sticks his head out the door, holding his own cell to his ear. "Hey, do you guys mind if my fiancée comes and hangs out?"

We all look around at each other, but none of us seem to care. His smile widens as he speaks into the phone.

"Get your ass down here, Bambi."

It takes a little bit for Knox to get the stencil created due to the size and the detail of it, but he manages. He comes out holding the transparent paper, a printout of the image, and Viola's phone. He hands the phone back to me and nods for me to come around the counter and over to his station.

Kage follows closely behind me, but I expected nothing different. Nico and *Ellis* make themselves at home, lounging on the couch that sits on the wall nearest where I'll be lying all night. Knox takes everything out and then turns to me.

"All right, whenever you're ready, you can take your shirt and bra off," he says.

Kage growls like a goddamn lion ready to rip him to shreds for the mere suggestion. Knox doesn't frighten easily though as he looks up at him.

"It's a back piece on her *upper* back," he explains. "There is literally no other solution except her taking her clothes off. But she'll be lying face down."

"Close your eyes," Kage demands. "And if you even so much as peek until I say you can open them, I'll rip your heart straight from your chest."

"You'd have to beat me to it," a voice says from behind us.

I turn around expecting to see someone just as tattooed as he is, maybe with a nose or eyebrow piercing and dressed in black, but that's not at all what I find. The girl has brown hair with a pair of sunglasses pushed up on the crown of her head. The white top she's wearing looks like something Viola or I would buy, and she's got a simple pair of blue jeans on.

She's honestly the complete *opposite* of what I pictured.

Knox looks at her and smiles as he stands up. "I'll do you one better, big guy. I'll leave the room completely." He walks over and grabs the woman's hand, pulling her into the back room. "Let me know when you're ready."

His fiancée giggles as they disappear, and it's adorable, until I see Kage's attention focused solely on me.

"You have to sit topless for the next however many hours as this fucker tattoos your back?" he growls lowly.

I lift one shoulder and tilt my head to the side. "I mean, yeah, but you'll be here, and so will his fiancée."

He clearly isn't happy, but he sighs and comes closer to help me get my shirt off without ruining my wig. Just as I go to pull the shirt up, he stops me.

"Nico, go stand in the corner," he demands.

Nico scoffs. "What? Seriously? I can't just close my eyes?"

"Did I fucking stutter?" he shouts. "Go stand in the goddamn corner."

Like a kid having a temper tantrum, he grumbles to himself as he gets up and marches into the corner. It takes a few moments for me to take the shirt and bra off, and then a few more for me to lie face down on the table and get situated so nothing is showing, but we manage. Kage walks around me in a circle to make sure nothing is visible, and then nods in approval.

"Okay!" I call for Knox. "We're ready."

He comes out with his fiancée in tow and smiles. "Great. Guys, this is my friend, Delaney."

She rolls her eyes and smacks him in the stomach. "You literally have my name inked on your chest with a marriage proposal."

"Aww!" I coo. "That's so cute."

Knox narrows his eyes on her. "Why do you have to make me look sappy at work? I'm supposed to be a badass."

Delaney gives him an *okay* look and nods. "Such a badass."

He pouts for a second but recovers when she kisses his neck. Then he's right back to being himself. Draping an arm around Delaney and holding her close, he points, starting with Kage.

"This is Kage, Viola, Nico, and Ellis." Viola is too sucked into her phone to notice as he whispers loud enough for us all to hear. "Ellis is special ed."

"She's special, not deaf," I quip.

Delaney looks over at Viola and smiles, seeming like a sweetheart. "I like your shoes, Ellis."

But she doesn't even react, still scrolling on her phone. Knox cocks a brow at me.

"You sure?"

I roll my eyes and look over at Viola. "Ellis?" Still nothing. "Ellis!"

Finally she snaps out of it. "Fuck. What?"

"I said I like your shoes," Delaney repeats.

Viola looks down at her shoes and then smiles. "Oh, thanks!"

As her attention goes back to her phone, we all share a look of pity. I should feel bad, but with everything she did *before* we were friends, I feel like it's karma catching up to her.

THE TATTOO TAKES OVER ten hours, and after the first two, my back goes numb with the exception of a few sensitive spots. I learn all about how Knox met *Bambi*, as he calls her, and how they fell in love despite being from opposite ends of the social spectrum. Viola and Nico wind up falling asleep on the couch halfway through, but Kage stays awake, watching Knox like a fucking hawk the whole time.

"Okay," Knox says, shutting off his tattoo gun and putting it down. "Let me just clean you up a bit and then you can take a look."

I feel a paper towel rub at my back and then I'm given the go-ahead to get up. Kage stands, blocking both Knox and Nico's view of me as I push myself up and use my T-shirt to cover my chest. I walk over to the mirror and admire my new ink.

The large, black angel wings are a stark contrast to my olive skin, but they're such a perfect representation of what I've been through lately that I know I made the right choice.

"I love it," I breathe.

Knox grins, proud of his work. "You look like a total badass."

And even better, I feel like one, too.

WHILE THE DRIVE TO Rhode Island made me question my sanity and vow never to take another road trip with Nico and Viola, the drive home is much quieter. The two in the back seat sleep almost the whole three and a half hours, while I drift in and out.

"Where are we?" Viola questions sleepily, rubbing her eyes.

"Almost to Long Island," I answer. "Did you have a nice nap, Ellis?"

She huffs and flops back against the seat. "Ugh. I told you, the one tattoo reminded me of Grey's Anatomy."

"And the first name you thought of wasn't Meredith?" I wave her off. "That's it. We can't be friends anymore."

Chuckling, she wraps her arms around me from the backseat. "Too bad you're stuck with me."

A few minutes later, we pull up to Raff's and the twins get out of the car. Viola stretches before half-heartedly waving goodbye, and Nico follows behind her like he's got a bad hangover. Kage looks over at me and smiles tiredly.

"You good?"

I nod. "My back is a little sore, but I had a lot of fun."

"Good," he says, putting his hand on the shifter and going to put the car in reverse, but before he can back out of the driveway, a scream sends a chill down both our spines.

He throws the car back into park, and the two of us move

at once, jumping out of the car and rushing up the stairs. The moment we get inside, we're faced with a scene from a goddamn horror movie. Viola is on her knees, screaming at the top of her lungs, while Nico stands there, in shock and shaking.

Raff sits in a recliner in the middle of the room. His eyes and mouth are wide open, as if he was frozen in fear. His skin is pale apart from the bruising around his throat, and the blood that comes from the six gunshots in his chest that match Kage's tattoos.

My heart shatters as the reality sets in.

Raff is dead.

CHAPTER 14

KAGE

EVERYTHING MOVES IN SLOW MOTION. I CAN FEEL my blood heating to a boil as I stare at the man who has been a father to me longer than my own was. Viola doesn't stop screaming and sobbing as she grabs at his hand, like it will somehow make him come back to life. Nico is stuck in a trance with tears flowing down his face as he stays completely unmoving.

I take a step toward the body and look at the holes that puncture his torso the same way they did my father. In only a few seconds, I can practically see a replay of what happened. They strangled him to death and then disrespected his corpse by firing six bullets into him, in the exact places my father was shot.

This was a message meant for me.

Devastation is not something I feel often, but lately it seems as if it's becoming my new normal. The pain in my chest as I fall to my knees in front of someone I loved and respected is overwhelming. I had always thought that if Dmitri was going to retaliate, he would come after me, but that was naive. He won't come for me because he knows he can't *beat* me.

So he preys on those closest to me.

A hand resting on my shoulder has me turning my head, and panic shoots through me as my gaze locks with Saxon's. At some point in the last twenty-four hours, Dmitri and his men were here. They left him here like this with the intention of me seeing it, and now Saxon is standing in the same spot.

They could be watching.

No.

She can't be here.

"We have to get you out of here," I say, standing up and grabbing her wrist.

As we head to the door, Viola chokes on her sobs. "Where are you going?"

I turn back and look her in the eyes. The pain she's feeling is one I understand more than one person should. She's breaking inside, and I get it.

"I will be right back. I promise."

She nods, and I quickly drag Saxon out of the house, practically tossing her into the car. I slam the door shut and march around to the driver's side. I throw the car into reverse and peel out of the driveway. Within seconds, I'm speeding down the road.

My fingers fumble with the buttons on the screen as I call Beni.

"Hey, Boss," he answers.

"I need you to send Roman over to Raff's house immediately," I order. "Then meet me at the halfway point between his place and mine. No public locations. Just the side of the road."

The sound of his keys jingling fill the background. "I'm on it. Is everything okay?"

"No," I tell him, and the next words that come out of my

mouth are ones I never thought I'd be saying so soon. "Raff was murdered."

I hang up immediately after and glance in the rearview mirrors, making sure we're not being followed. Saxon watches me carefully, but I can't look back at her right now, because she's the one who makes me face my emotions, and right now, the only thing I'm able to focus on is getting her back to my place, where I know she's safe.

Five minutes later, I spot Beni in my blacked-out Mercedes speeding toward me. We both slam on our brakes, and he spins around to my side of the road.

"Kage," Saxon pleads. "Say something."

Her cheeks are wet with tears as I finally turn to her. "I need you to get in the car with Beni, and I need you to stay at home until I get there."

She's clearly battling between agreeing and fighting me on it, wanting to be there to support me, but she nods anyway. The two of us get out of the car, and I place my hand on her lower back as I walk her over to Beni.

"Take her straight back to my house and stay with her. Don't let her out of your sight," I tell him.

He nods and opens the passenger door for her. Before she can get in, she spins back around and presses a kiss to my lips, one that almost feels like she's afraid this could be the last time she sees me. Either that or she just knows how badly I need it right now.

I get back in the SUV and watch as Beni speeds off toward home. I put the car back in drive and spin around, heading back to Raff's house. It feels like an out of body experience, as if I've done this so many times, I'm on autopilot. The instructions on how to isolate the pain caused by losing a parent are hardwired into my brain, and I can't tell if that's good or bad.

When I get back, I toss the car into park and jump out. Roman is already inside, standing with his hand on Raff's shoulder and a devastated look on his face. Despite the fact that Raff betrayed the Familia, he was still a father figure to us all for a long time.

"Call Dante and get him over here," I tell Ro.

He nods and heads into the back of the house to make the call. Viola is still sitting on the floor sobbing, while Nico is on the couch with his face in his hands. I walk over and squat down in front of the body, putting my hand on his knee.

"Fuck, Raff," I breathe. "Goddamn it."

Spending a little over a decade as the Don of the Familia, Raff wasn't a man who couldn't defend himself. When he ruled, he was ruthless. It took me years to learn from him, and I don't know what I would've done without his guidance.

They had to have overpowered him. Ambushed him when he least expected it and didn't give him a chance at fighting them off. Dmitri is a coward who relies on others to do his dirty work, so it wouldn't surprise me if he had his goons strangle him before he fired the shots into his torso.

I shake my head, not wanting to believe he's gone. "I hope you, Silas, and my dad are partying it up, reunited again."

I'M STANDING OUTSIDE WITH Roman as Dante and

his men carry Raff out in a body bag. I'm not going to sugarcoat it—it's a hard thing to see. I always imagined he'd live well into his nineties, sitting in his recliner and still choosing to watch TV shows in black and white. Instead, he was ripped away from us like so many others before him.

"If Dmitri thought I was after him before," I growl lowly, "his mind can't even dream of what I'm going to do to him now."

Ro nods, taking a paper out of his pocket. "I found this taped to the back of Raff's neck."

I grab the small piece of paper and read it over.

Look familiar, Kagey-boy?
Guess I wasn't next after all.
- D.P.

My anger spikes once more, and I crumble the note in my hand. "This means war. I don't care if I have to kill every goddamn Bratva I come across. I want to wear his intestines as a necklace of honor."

WALKING THROUGH THE FRONT door of my house, I'm exhausted and wide awake all at the same time. Saxon runs across the foyer and crashes against my chest, wrapping her arms around me. Beni follows behind her and gives me a sad smile.

"He make it to the funeral home safely?" he questions.

I nod. "Roman is staying there tonight. Cesari will take tomorrow."

It's customary in the Familia that those who die in honor get looked after until they're laid to rest. I followed the hearse the whole way from Raff's house, making sure that Dmitri and his fuckwits didn't try anything to destroy the body in transit. Roman rode with me, and when we got there, he nodded respectfully and walked inside behind the funeral staff with Raff.

"If you don't need me, I'd like to take tomorrow night," he requests.

"I'll allow it," I tell him. "Roman will take your place here. I just need you to stay with Saxon tomorrow during the day while I take care of a few things."

"Absolutely."

Saxon buries her face into my chest, breathing me in, and in a way, it helps. But just like when she woke up in the hospital, I can feel parts of me closing off. And the result is the same.

The only thing that will help me heal is getting my hands on Dmitri and ripping him limb from limb.

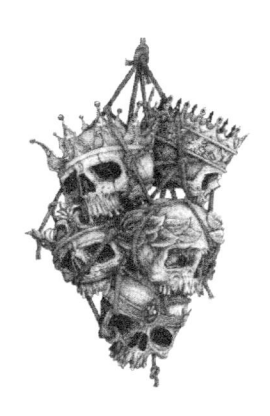

ONE OF THE HARDEST parts of losing someone is having to feel that loss over and over again as you deliver the news to their loved ones. It's as if you're in a perpetual loop of grief and misery as you mentally relive the moment part of your world died. And this time will be no different.

Viola holds her head high as she walks beside me into the facility. There isn't a single tear in her eyes, telling me she pushed it all down and numbed herself to it. She's like me in that regard. We're stronger when we refuse to acknowledge the pain.

"You ready?" I ask her as we stop outside of the room.

She chuckles dryly. "Ready or not, here we go."

Turning the corner, I see the woman who stood by Raff's side for so many years. Cecilia has always been a beautiful woman. Even at her age, with her mix of gray and blonde hair that goes down to her shoulders, you can tell she was a knockout in her day.

"Hey Mom," Viola greets her, a note of hope in her voice.

Cecilia looks up at us both, and Viola's shoulders sag as it becomes obvious there's no recollection in her mother's eyes. "Oh, hello."

Vi glances back at me, shaking her head in disappointment. She didn't mention it, but I knew she was hoping her mom would be lucid for this conversation. Otherwise, there's virtually no point in having it. With her early-onset dementia, she won't remember a thing.

I remember when it started. Raff tried everything in his power to take care of her. He asked for permission to step away from any duties he had to the Familia so he could be her full-time caregiver. I granted his request without hesitation, but when she got worse, it was too much for him to handle. It reached a point where he was jeopardizing her safety by having her at home. After the morning she lit a fire in the kitchen after forgetting the stove was on, he decided to make the difficult decision to put her in an assisted living facility.

And her brain has only deteriorated from there.

The bouts of lucidity became shorter and less often until she completely forgot who we all were. But he still came every day and brought her a single rose for her vase. He'd read her the news like he used to do when they'd drink their coffee in the morning, and then he'd kiss her forehead and leave.

"Do you still want to tell her?" I murmur softly to Viola.

She sighs. "No. We'll wait until the day she's lucid, if that day ever comes."

I nod in understanding as my phone vibrates in my pocket. I pull it out, seeing Mattia's name on the screen.

"Excuse me while I take this," I murmur and step out of the room.

Taking a calming breath, I look up and down the hall before pressing the phone to my ear.

"What?"

Mattia's voice has a sorrowful tone to it. "I heard about Raff and wanted to express my deepest condolences to you and your family."

I scoff. "Yeah, well, while you're at it, maybe you could explain to me how this man managed to get inside Raff's house and kill him while I'm paying you and Costello thousands of dollars an hour to find the son of a bitch."

"He's a difficult guy to track down," he explains. "Almost never shows his face and only travels in the dead of night. It was even rumored he was on a flight back to Russia after Vlad's death. There was no way we could have seen this coming. I'm sorry."

"I don't want your excuses, Mattia," I growl. "What I want is Dmitri's location so I can rip his jugular straight from his throat. I don't care what it takes or if you don't sleep a wink for three days straight. Make it fucking happen."

Just as I hang up the phone, Viola steps out into the hall. She runs her fingers through her hair, looking like she's both numb and barely holding it together all at once. She glances back at her mother before looking at me.

"I don't know what we're going to do," she says honestly. "This place is expensive, and Nico and I can't care for her in her condition."

I put my hands on her shoulders to stop her. "Don't worry about that. She's family, and she will be taken care of as such."

Tears fill her eyes as she nods and wraps her arms around my waist. Usually I would shove her off me. Showing compassion isn't something I do unless the person happens to have black hair, blue eyes, and an unmatched ability to drive me insane. But all Raff wanted while he was alive was for us to be there for each other like siblings, and the least I can do is give him that while we all mourn his loss.

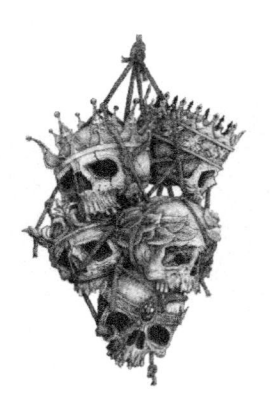

WHEN YOU THINK OF a funeral, you tend to picture dreary weather with cloud-covered skies and a wind chill that makes you shiver. But not Raff's. The sun shines brightly over his casket, making it so all of us can feel its warmth. I can't help but wonder if that was his doing. Unfortunately, if his intention was to change my mood, it isn't working.

My men and I all stand together, our heads bowed in respect as we listen to the priest talk about what a great businessman Raff was and how much his family meant to him. A picture of him with my father and Silas sits to the side of the casket, broad smiles on all of their faces. I hope they're as happy now as they were then.

Glancing to the side, I notice Scarlett standing off to the side. She's dressed in all black, like the rest of us, holding a small black clutch in front of her. I want to watch her, to get a feel for what is going through her head, but as Viola steps up to the podium to speak, my attention is pulled away. She stands there, looking like a pillar of strength, with her brown hair pinned back. Taking a deep breath, she looks down at the paper and back up at the crowd.

"My father was a noble man. To his friends, he was loyal. To his family, he was dependable. Anyone who really knew him knows that he was always there to listen. If he could do anything to help, he would do it. It didn't matter who you were.

"I remember the time my prom date was late to pick me up. Being a seventeen year old girl, dramatics were my specialty. Five minutes after he was supposed to show up, I wasn't telling myself reasonable things like car trouble or just running a bit late. I was stomping around the house, calling him every name under the sun for standing me up. Dad talked shit about him with me for a half hour, before the doorbell rang and there was my prom date. Turns out the limo was just late picking him up, and I hadn't checked my phone."

The crowd chuckles before she continues.

"My parents were the ideal couple. The thing you picture when you read romance novels. He put her first every single day from the moment they met. And when they had Nico and me, he did the same with us. I can't remember a single time that I needed something and he wasn't there to help me. What I can remember, however, is the time he came home and told me that we were getting a new brother. His best friend had passed away, leaving his ten-year-old son an orphan. But Dad wouldn't have that. And when I threw a fit and asked him why I had to share a room with Nico, he bent down, looked me in the eyes, and said that we're family, and family takes care of its own."

She looks over at me and I give her a small smile, nodding once in respect.

"As we lay to rest the man who was a father figure to so many, the one thing I hope you feel when you think of him is the warmth that he spread wherever he went." She turns her head toward the casket and wipes a tear from her cheek. "And don't worry, Dad. I'll have the Giants game on for you this Sunday."

Ending her speech, she walks over and places a rose on top of his casket. Nico goes next, quietly holding his hand on the wood for a moment before taking a step back. As I step up, I place two roses down beside Viola's—one for me, and one for Saxon. After that, everyone else gets their turn to pay their respects, but as the funeral starts to come to an end, I find my anger building by the second.

Rage flows through my veins, charring everything in its path, the fire inside of me being suffocated until it's nothing but glowing embers. My fist clenches as I listen to those around me cry their fake tears, whispering about age old memories they wouldn't have remembered if not for the current circumstance. And when they lower the casket into the ground, the last honorable part of me goes along with it.

Nothing but malice remains.

And mark my words.

I'm going to find Dmitri.

And I'm going to skin him alive.

Everything comes to a close, and I glance over at where Scarlett stood, but she's already walking away. I push past a few people, murmuring insincere apologies as I try to follow her. Nothing good can come of this, though I can't find it in me to care.

But divine intervention must have other plans.

A grip on my wrist has me turning around to see Nico standing there, a furious glare focused on me. To say he hasn't been the same since the day we found Raff would be an understatement. Viola has been keeping an eye on him, but he's been an empty shell of a man.

"Give me a minute," I tell him. "I'll be right back."

"No!" he roars. "Fuck you!"

"Nico!" Viola shouts as my brows raise.

"Excuse me?"

He puts his hands on my chest and pushes me as hard as he can. "You fucking heard me. You did this!"

I take a minute, reminding myself that he's grieving and

not in his right mind. "How about we have this conversation elsewhere?"

"Why? So that everyone doesn't know you're the reason he's dead?" he snaps. "If you weren't on a goddamn power trip, they wouldn't have come after him! You may as well have shot him yourself!"

Putting a hand up, I glance around. "Lower your tone before I lower it for you."

Clearly taking orders isn't something he's willing to do right now, as he rears back and punches me directly in the jaw. My men act at once, rushing to grab us both, but not before I get a couple hits of my own in. As I'm pulled back, I touch my lip and see that I'm bleeding.

Beni keeps a hand on my chest as I point at Nico with my index and middle fingers together. "We just put the only man who ever kept me from killing you in the ground. I suggest you don't fucking cross me again."

He says nothing, just takes rapid breaths through his nose as he glares at me.

I spin on my heels and force myself to walk away before I toss Raff's prized moron into the grave with him.

Chapter 15

Saxon

Everyone handles grief differently. Some like to reminisce, thinking about the good times and how they're in a better place. While others, like myself, need to burn in it. It sets us on fire from the inside and chips away at pieces of us, taking what it wants with reckless abandon. Kage is the same.

He's been cold—dead inside like I was—and I can't say I blame him. He already lost his parents at such a young age. Having to relive that with Raff at thirty-four was just the icing on his trauma cake. But that doesn't mean I don't want to do whatever it takes to help him. After all, he did the same for me.

I pace back and forth across the floor as I wait for him to get back from the funeral. I'd be staring out the window if it wasn't for the two guards standing out front. They think the house is empty, and if they saw the *supposed to be dead* girl in the window, they'd either shit themselves or come busting through the door.

I'd rather not find out which it would be.

It's half past noon when he finally comes in the door. My socks slip against the floor as I jump off the couch and rush to get to him, but as I get closer, I come to halt. He looks like he's aged a hundred years in a single morning, and there's a new cut on his lip that wasn't there when he left.

"What the fuck happened?" I ask, putting my hand on his cheek.

"It's fine," he says, tossing his suit jacket on the chair by the door. "Nothing you should concern yourself with."

Taking his hand, I lead him over to the couch. He sits down, and I stand behind him as I massage his shoulders. Lately, it's as if he's been holding the weight of the world. From losing the mafia properties to my near-death experience and losing our baby, and now to this. It's bound to reach a point where he just snaps, and I just hope I'm able to bring him back from the edge before he goes over.

I lean forward, sliding my hands down his chest and undoing the buttons one at a time as I kiss his neck. At first he stays silent, but once I get my hands on his skin, he hums. Moving my lips to the shell of his ear, I whisper the same thing he told me. The one thing that helped keep me from my breaking point.

"Take it out on me."

He turns to look at me, a delicious smirk splayed across his face. "You don't know what you're asking for."

"Try me," I say confidently. "As hard as you want. As rough as you need. Take it out on me."

Taking my wrist, he pulls me around the side of the couch and into his lap. "I'll end up hurting you."

"I can take it."

Before he can argue further, I press my lips to his in a bruising kiss. His hands move to my hips, and when I grind down against him, he sucks in a breath of air. As if I'm weightless, he picks me up and carries me into the bedroom, kicking the door shut behind him and tossing me onto the bed.

His eyes stay locked with mine as he undoes his belt and lets it fall to the floor. He pushes his pants and boxers down in one go and takes his cock into his hands, jerking it a few times.

"All right, Gabbana," he says, looking from me to his dick and back again. "Do your fucking worst."

Crawling across the bed to the edge, I lick my lips as I take him in my hand. I don't think I'll ever get over how big he is. Even my hand can't fit all the way around. I look up at him through my lashes as I kiss the tip.

He laces his fingers into my hair and tugs just enough to cause a slight pain. "If I wanted a hand job, I would've done it myself. Open your goddamn mouth and suck me like you need it."

My core tightens, and I clench around nothing at his words. Doing as he says, I stick my tongue out and wrap my lips around his cock. He throws his head back as I swallow around him.

"Fuck."

I've always heard that blowjobs were work. Nessa always complained about them, like they were a one-way street, with all give and no get, but Kage is something else. The sounds he makes and the way he gets even harder inside my mouth only turns me on more.

I take as much of him in as I can, sliding him in and out, but it's not enough. He gathers all of my hair and holds it as if it's a handle. He holds my head in place as he thrusts forward, forcing himself into the back of my throat and groaning as I choke on it. As he pulls back, a trail of saliva goes from his dick to my mouth, but before I can wipe it away, he harshly pushes back in.

"Jesus Christ, your mouth," he groans.

My eyes water as I gag on his cock. This is what he needs,

to use every inch of my body for whatever he sees fit, and I'm fucking loving it. Watching him treat me like I'm indestructible is such a fucking turn-on.

When he's had enough, he pulls out and lies down on the bed, stroking himself slowly.

"Get up and strip for me," he orders. "I want to see what's mine."

I stand from the bed and grab the bottom of my shirt, slowly pulling it up and over my head. Sliding my hands down over my heated skin, my fingers dip into the waistband of my jeans. I turn around as I slide them down my legs, leaving me in only my bra and thong.

Kage's gaze stays on me, burning into my skin as I unclip my bra and slide the straps down my arms. I look back to see him biting his lip.

"Turn around and show me those perfect tits."

I do as he says, rubbing my hands over my breasts and feeling as my nipples harden.

He grips himself tighter and moans. "That's it. Play with them just for me."

My hands squeeze them lightly as I throw my head back. I roll each nipple between my thumb and index finger. I'm so fucking needy that my legs are shaking. When Kage notices, he slides down on the bed until he's lying flat.

"Get over here and sit on my face," he says. "I'm fucking starving."

Sliding my thong down my legs and kicking it away, I climb onto the bed. Kage grabs my hips and lifts me over him before lowering me down. The second his mouth is on me, my every nerve ending ignites. He licks and sucks me with fervor, using his grip on my waist to pull me down harder.

The pressure starts to become too much and not enough all at once. I slide my fingers into his hair and use my grip to pull him closer. He groans against me, the vibration making everything that much more intense.

"That's it, baby. Ride my face. Use me like I used you."

And I do. I grind down against him like I'll die if I don't. And honestly? I might. The need to orgasm is so intense my core becomes impossibly tight just as my movements become frantic. Kage knows I'm getting close and reaches up, putting his hands on my shoulders and pulling me against him.

My orgasm crashes into me like a freight train, my whole body convulses uncontrollably as I scream. Kage doesn't stop for a second, making it last as long as possible. When I finally start to come down from my high, he gives one last kitten lick—teasing me for how I teased him.

Gripping my waist, he moves me down his body until I'm hovering over his dick, and just like that, I'm ready to come all over again. As I take all of him inside of me, I moan at the sensation of fullness. The fact that he manages to fit completely inside of me is amazing. I could keep him deep inside me like this for the rest of my life and not have a single complaint.

"Goddamn," he moans, pressing his head into the pillow. "That's a good girl. So fucking needy for me."

"Fuck, Kage."

"Yes. Scream my fucking name so everyone knows who you belong to."

"All yours," I promise him as I ride his cock. "All fucking yours."

I bounce on his cock, shoving my tits in his face. He teases my nipples with his talented tongue. And when I feel like I'm starting to get close again, I grind down on him, taking all of him and loving the way he fills every inch of me.

He takes two fingers and puts them to my lips. "Suck."

Opening my mouth, he shoves them inside and I coat them with my saliva. When he pulls them out, he reaches around and rubs over my puckered hole. Slowly, like torture, he pushes his index finger in to the first knuckle.

"I told you one day I was going to take this hole, too," he murmurs.

My breath hitches as I realize what he's insinuating. Excitement starts to build in my stomach as I push back against his finger, stretching around him. He starts to work me open. He uses one finger until he's thrusting it into me, and only when I'm begging for it does he add another.

Two is a much bigger stretch than one, but as his cock fills my pussy, his fingers add to the pressure. It's fucking intoxicating. In a scissor-like motion, he gets my ass ready to take his cock. The sensation of it all is out of this world, and I feel as the pressure starts to build.

"Yeah?" he asks as he sees I'm almost there. "You like when my fingers are in your ass, don't you?"

"I do," I murmur, nodding.

He shoves a third one in and smirks when it only pushes me further. "Just wait until it's my fucking cock."

That's all it takes to send me soaring into orgasm central. I'm so sensitive everywhere, and it's fucking incredible. I drop my forehead against his as my pussy clenches around him so tight.

Kage doesn't miss a beat. The second my orgasm starts to slow, he slides his fingers out and flips me onto my back. His thrusts are hard and fast, taking no mercy and only getting him harder until he pulls out and lines up at my ass.

"I want you to take a deep breath, and then let it out slow," he tells me.

Doing what he says, I inhale until my lungs can't take anymore, and as I start to let it out, he presses into me. Pain is everywhere, but it's a good kind of hurt. His dick is so much bigger than his fingers, but the stretch is everything.

"Oh my God," I breathe.

He looks down, admiring the way his cock looks in my ass as he slowly pushes further in. His thumb rubs against my sensitive clit to distract me from the feeling of him damn near splitting me open. And it works.

By the time he bottoms out, I'm a panting mess, overwhelmed by the pressure. He stays completely still for a moment. His eyes stay locked on mine as he waits for me to adjust.

"Move," I tell him.

He smirks. "Yes, ma'am."

Starting off slow, he pulls out to the head and then thrusts all the way back in. It takes a minute to get used to, but the faster he goes, the better it feels. His grip on my hips is so tight I know there are going to be bruises left behind in the morning.

"Holy fuck," he growls.

I lace my fingers into my own hair while he fucks my ass just as hard as he fucks my pussy. His jaw locks as he starts to get closer, chasing his own high while my third is fiercely approaching. Getting better leverage, he uses his hands to pull me onto him rather than thrusting into me, and the angle hits just right.

"I'm going to fill you up so good. You want my cum in your ass?"

"Yes!" I scream as I get closer. "Cum in my ass. I want it all."

His movements quicken as he fucks me harder, taking us both over the edge. He shoves two fingers into my pussy and crooks them just right. Animalistic sounds fill the air as we let go and he empties everything he has into my ass.

The two of us are drenched in sweat, and I wince as he slowly pulls out. He crashes down next to me and presses a quick kiss to my lips, then smiles.

"You really were fucking made for me."

I SIT ON THE couch with Kage's head in my lap, running my fingers through his hair as he types out an email on his phone. Mattia and Costello, the other private investigator Kage hired, have been working tirelessly to find Dmitri with no luck, much to Kage's fury. And judging by the way Beni and Roman marched into the office before, I'm guessing they're all losing patience.

The clock is ticking, and it's only a matter of time before Mauricio calls with the news that ownership of my grandfather's properties has been transferred over to my prick of a father. If they don't get to Dmitri before that, they'll lose everything to the Bratva. Control of the city will be theirs, and I will have to watch as Kage feels like a failure, despite how hard he's fought for the Familia.

"Oh, shit," Roman's voice echoes from the office. "Incoming!"

The front door opens with such force that it slams against the wall and almost shuts itself. Kage is up off the couch in seconds, pulling out his gun and pointing it toward the door until Viola appears. He and I both exhale and he puts his gun away.

"Jesus Christ, Viola. I almost killed you," he says.

"Wouldn't be the first time," she snaps back.

Her attitude doesn't go unnoticed as he looks her up and down. "What's your problem?"

"Funny you should ask." She puts her hand on her hip. "I just had to watch as our brother trashed the entire house in an angry rage."

Kage grunts. "Okay, first of all, that's *your* brother, not mine. And second, why is this my problem?"

"Because your little argument at the funeral is what sent him off the deep end!"

"Please," he scoffs, pointing to the cut on his lip. "He's the one that hit me."

My eyes widen in concern. "Wait, *Nico* did that to you?"

They both ignore me as Viola glares at Kage. "You knew he hasn't been himself since Dad died. And what do you do? You go and banish him from the only family he has left."

"He's fucking lucky that's all I did!" he sneers. "I should've shot him in the head for what he did!"

"If he keeps up like this, you won't have to," she yells. "He'll do it himself, and that death *will* be on you."

I can see Kage is starting to get angry. Both their emotions are high, and they're taking their stressful day out on each other. I jump off the couch and put myself between them.

"Okay, Vi," I say calmly, understanding that she's grieving. "That's a little uncalled for."

She looks like she's going to snap at me next, but then she stops and takes a deep breath. "I'm sorry. It's just that Nico looks up to you, Kage. He has since we were kids, you just never paid attention enough to see it. And I don't want to see him lose everything because of something he said when he was dealing with the death of our father. You of all people should know what that kind of grief does to a person."

Instead of saying anything, he turns and walks away, going into our bedroom and slamming the door behind him. Viola plops down onto the couch and covers her face with her hands. I glance at the bedroom door, knowing he would've taken me with him if he wanted me in there. So, I sit next to Viola and wrap my arms around her.

"It's been a tough few days, for *all* of us," I tell her. "Give him some time. Nico, too. Men are stubborn, but they'll come around. Whether Kage wants to admit it or not, you're family."

She wipes a stray tear from her face and sniffles. "I really hope you're right, because I can't handle losing them, too."

I WAKE IN THE middle of the night, rolling over to find the other side of the bed empty and cold. Glancing at the alarm clock, I read the time. *3:37 a.m.* I sit up and rub my eyes with my fists. I'm not going to be able to fall back asleep without knowing he's okay.

As I get out of bed, I grab the blanket and wrap it around my naked body. The hardwood floor feels cold against my feet. I leave the bedroom in search of Kage and immediately find that the living room is empty. Not even Beni is sitting on the couch, which is good because Kage would lose his mind if he saw me this way.

The light coming from Kage's office gives away his location, but when I get to the doorway, it's not at all what I expected to find. Kage is sitting at his desk with a half-empty bottle of Cognac, not even drinking from a glass—opting for straight out of the bottle.

"Hey," I greet him softly.

He looks up at me, and I can already see the gloss that coats his eyes. "Hi Gabbana."

"You okay?" I ask. "Drinking in the middle of the night isn't normally your style."

Smiling sadly, he shrugs. "I don't know."

My heart hurts for him as I realize what this is about. "Viola told me what Nico said at the funeral."

Kage grabs the bottle to take another sip, but I grab it from him and carefully put it back down on the desk.

"It's not true," I tell him honestly.

He exhales, looking anywhere but back at me as I turn his chair and place myself in his lap. I've seen so many different emotions in Kage.

Anger.

Jealousy.

Fear.

But this one is different.

My head turns toward his desk, and I notice he has a picture of him and Raff at his high school graduation on the screen. They look happy, with Raff's arm tightly around him as they smile at the camera. It's a picture that should be cherished, and yet he's using it for something else entirely.

"Hey." I put a hand on his cheek and his eyes lock with mine. "I love you."

He exhales, the corners of his mouth twitching upward. "I love you, too."

"Then tell me," I say softly. "Are you mad because Nico blamed you, or because deep down, you blame yourself, too?"

CHAPTER 16

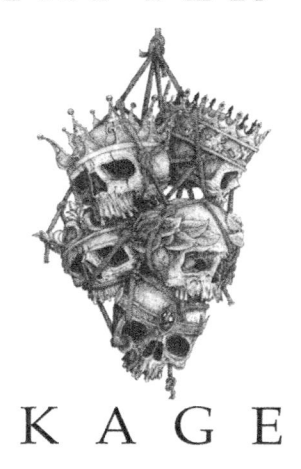

KAGE

Darkness has a way of creeping up on you. It gets under your skin, wrapping itself around your veins and injecting itself into your bloodstream. The longer it goes, the more it intensifies, until you're clawing at your own skin just to remind yourself you're alive.

It's like the plague, and the cure is having Dmitri at my mercy—hanging in front of me so I can inflict all the pain he deserves.

He knows we're searching for him. He'd be naive to think I'm not using everything in my power to find him. He knows, and he's fucking loving it. It's like the thrill of the chase, only reversed. The reason why he hasn't run back to Russia until the properties are ready for transfer is because he's getting off on this game of cat and mouse.

I hold the phone to my ear, my grip tightening by the second. "Why the fuck haven't you found him yet?"

Mattia swallows so harshly I can hear it through the phone. "I'm sorry, sir. He must be taking extra precautions not to be found. I can assure you that we've been working day in and day out."

"Extend the search," I order. "Any Bratva you see, I want to know about it. I don't care about their rank or their social status. You see one, you send me their location."

"Yes, sir. Absolutely, sir."

I hang up the phone and slam it down on my desk before the response is finished coming out of his mouth. Saxon walks in, with sweat glistening across her skin as she just finished her training with Ralph.

"You okay?" she asks as she comes closer. "You look frustrated."

I grab her and pull her into my lap. "How do you feel about a little more practice before you deliver your revenge? Because it's about to get messy around here."

Like the violent little vixen she's become, her grin widens and she nods excitedly, as if I just gave her the greatest gift of all.

IT DOESN'T TAKE LONG before we're called with a location. It's no one of importance, but just being a part of the Bratva organization makes him a target of mine. On my orders, Roman grabs Cesari and the two of them go to pick him up.

"Anything new on Nico?" I ask Beni as we wait.

He shakes his head. "We've got someone at the house at all times, but he's been cooped up in the house all week. If it wasn't for the twice a day that he comes down stairs to get food, we'd start to wonder if he's dead."

The day after the funeral, I decided to put someone at Raff's old house for multiple reasons. For one, they need the protection. Dmitri has been there once before, and I wouldn't put it past him to go again looking to kill one of them. Out of respect for Raff, I won't leave them unprotected. The other reason is that Nico is one of few who know that Saxon is still alive, and with how unhinged he was at the funeral, I can't take any chances with him blabbing about that to the wrong person.

"And Viola?"

He puts his hand out and rocks it from side to side. "Some days are better than others, but she's hanging in there."

"Wait," Saxon interrupts us. "Turn that up."

I look over at the TV, and my nostrils flare as I see Dalton's picture on the screen. The headline on the bottom reads *Forbes Penthouse For Sale*. Beni turns the volume up and the three of us listen intently.

"The penthouse belonging to the Forbes family is up for sale after it became too hard for Dalton and Scarlett Forbes to keep living there after the tragic death of their daughter, Saxon," the newscaster reports. "One of our own caught up with Dalton earlier to ask him about the decision to move, and this is what he had to say…"

The screen switches to footage of Dalton exiting the building with his briefcase in hand as the reporter runs alongside him for a comment.

"Mr. Forbes, is it true you listed your penthouse for sale?"

Dalton nods. "It is. Are you interested?"

The female interviewer chuckles. "I would be if I had your kind of money. You've lived there for decades. What made you finally decide to move?"

Dalton stops and runs his fingers through his hair. "It was a necessary move. Losing Saxon has been very difficult for all of us to cope with, and it's too painful to live in the penthouse without her."

"I am so sorry for your loss," she tells him. "Have you bought another place in the city?"

He gives her his charming smile. "Uh, no comment."

"Very well. Thank you for speaking with me."

"You have a good day."

Switching back to the newscaster, they move onto another headline as Beni turns the volume back down. Saxon stays glaring at the screen long after her father's face disappears. Her hand is gripping the throw pillow so tight, it looks like she's about to rip it to shreds.

"I want nothing more than to cut that smug grin right off his face," she growls.

Beni turns to look at her with brows furrowed. "You mean *wipe* the smug grin off his face."

She stares back at him, shaking her head slowly with the same fire in her eyes I fell in love with. Beni glances between her and me, his smile growing.

"Careful, boss. I think she might end up more dangerous than you are."

I look down at Saxon and as her eyes meet mine, she relaxes into me. "There's no doubt in my mind about that."

And it's true, because while I was raised to kill, she was born for it. She can look anyone in the eyes and make them think she's their friend, right before she plunges a knife deep into their chest. It's that charm that makes her so lethal.

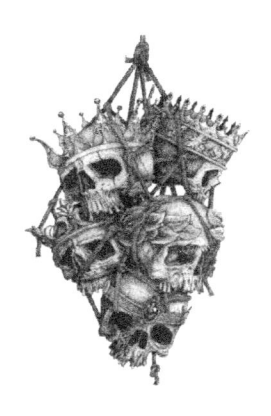

OVER THE COURSE OF a week, we go through five different Bratva scumbags—each one more useless than the last. No matter what we do to them, none will give up Dmitri's location. I'm starting to wonder if they're incredibly loyal, or if they genuinely just don't know where he is.

Catching a glance of Saxon in the backyard and one of our prisoners running around the back, I rush outside, but when I hear the silenced gunshots, my pace slows. I walk over to the ledge that overlooks the lawn portion of the yard and sit down, spreading my legs as my feet hang. Saxon is shooting at the Bratva prick, literally using him as target practice, and pride swells in my chest as I watch her.

"Your aim still sucks," I tease as she misses her second to last shot.

I thought Beni would have had better luck teaching her, but I'm thinking she may be useless when it comes to needing a gun.

She turns around with a look that could kill and points the gun, firing a shot that embeds itself in the wall only a couple inches below my dick. My eyes widen as I look at how close she was to castrating me and look back up at her. She smiles and winks at me.

Her aim is perfect.

I reach behind me and pull out my own gun. My gaze stays locked with Saxon as I point it over her shoulder and fire. She turns around just in time to see the guy fall to the ground—dead from a gunshot straight to the head.

"Kage!" she cries, stomping her foot. "What the hell did you do that for? You ruined my fun!"

Shrugging carelessly, I put my gun down next to me. "He had your attention. I didn't like it."

"Your greed knows no bounds."

I can't tell if she's really mad or just fucking with me. Still, she comes closer and stands in front of me, her arms resting on my shoulders while I place my hands on her hips. I pull her closer and press a kiss to her lips.

"Mine."

She rolls her eyes playfully. "Yes, Tarzan. All yours."

IT DOESN'T EVEN TAKE a full day before Roman brings us home another one. He's a mouthy little prick, but all he's doing is spewing insults at the moment. Though I would be, too, if someone had me tied up with a bag over my head.

"Where do you want him, boss?" Ro asks as he stands in the middle of the shed.

"The chair," Saxon tells him the same time I say to hang him.

With clashing opinions, Saxon and I turn to look at each other. She holds her head high, unwavering, and while normally I'd appease her, I don't have time. Time is dwindling, and there is no doubt that when Dmitri is finished with his business here, he'll be on the first flight back to Russia.

And international flights piss me off.

"We don't have time for you to play, Gabbana," I tell her. "We need answers."

She scoffs. "You can still question him while he's sitting. And besides, if you hadn't killed my last one, I wouldn't need this one. You owe me."

"And I'll make up for that later. But right now, this is business."

Instead of arguing further, she puts one hand out flat with her other in a fist on top of it. My brows furrow as I wonder if she's officially lost it.

"What are you doing?" I ask hesitantly.

She gets frustrated, grabbing my hands and doing the same thing with my own. "We're playing Rock, Paper, Scissors. Winner gets to go first."

Roman smirks as my answer becomes clear— she *has* officially lost it. "Absolutely not. I'm not playing some stupid kids game to *win* my way. Ro, hang him."

"*Ro*, wait," she counters.

I turn to Ro, looking at him expectantly, but he doesn't move. "With all due respect, Boss, she's mean. I'd really rather not be in the middle of this."

"Smart man," Saxon compliments him and then turns back to me. "Come on."

"For fuck's sake." I roll my eyes and hold out my fist. "You're a child. I hope you know that."

She smiles sarcastically. "And you're robbing the cradle.

Now that we've got *that* out of the way, let's do this. Best two out of three."

The two of us stand in the middle of a makeshift torture chamber and play Rock, Paper, Scissors while the guy thrashing in Roman's hold gets to hear us. She wins the first round and cheers for herself, but the second goes to me. The next round determines it all. We glare at each other as our fists bounce off our palms.

Rock.

Paper.

Scissors.

Shoot.

I throw out scissors, but as I look at Saxon and see her holding rock, I realize she won. She grins and arches up on her tiptoes, kissing my cheek and telling me good game, and then turns to Ro.

"In the chair, Roman my dear," she commands.

He does as she says, chaining the guy to the chair and making it so he can't move. As he goes to walk out, he pats my shoulder.

"Better luck next time."

I grunt. "Fuck off."

Saxon rips the bag from his head. His messy brown hair goes in all different directions as he whips his head around, trying to see where he is. When his eyes land on Saxon, he looks confused.

"Who are you?"

She pulls a chair up in front of them and takes a bottle of yellow nail polish out of her pocket. "I'm Gabbana, and we're going to be the best of friends."

He and I both watch her with bewilderment as she opens the polish and literally starts to paint his nails. She's been getting creative with her torture methods lately, but this time, even *I* don't know where she's going with it.

When neither one of us says anything, she looks up at me and gestures toward the Bratva. "Go ahead."

I pinch the bridge of my nose and exhale. "Listen. It can be as easy as what she's doing right now if you just tell me where Dmitri Petrov is hiding."

He snorts. "Yeah, okay."

"It can also get a lot worse if you don't."

He glances at where Saxon is carefully concentrated on making his nails look perfect. "I've seen the things he can do to someone for making his lunch wrong. I'd rather take my chances here."

"Gabbana," I growl.

She looks up at me. "What? I'm almost done."

The things I deal with for this woman, I swear. "Let me make myself very clear here. You aren't making it out of here alive if you don't tell me where he is."

"That's fair and all, but I won't live past tomorrow if I *do* tell you where he is. And judging by how this is going, I'm guessing you'll make it a lot less painful."

"There," Saxon says as she puts the applicator back in the bottle. "Okay, let me see."

The prick smiles as he pretends to proudly show her his nails, thinking she's completely unhinged, but he doesn't know the half of it. She purses her lips as she looks at them and then shakes her head.

"I don't like it."

Getting up, she goes over to the table and grabs a pair of needle-nose pliers. The Bratva can't see what she's doing, but I can, and pride swells inside my chest. She comes back to our victim and instead of taking off the nail polish, she starts to rip each one of his nails out. He's not expecting the first one, and I watch as his eyes widen before he wails in pain. No matter how much he tries to stop her, he can't. He's at her mercy as she pulls every single nail from his fingers.

When she's done, she stops to observe her handiwork

and grins. "Oh yes! Red is *much* more your color."

"You psychotic fucking bitch!" he screams.

I grab the baseball bat that hangs on the wall and swing it, striking him in the face. "That is a lady! God, what is wrong with all of you? Did your mothers teach you no manners?"

He spits blood and one of his teeth out onto the floor as he sneers at Saxon. "*That* is no fucking lady. That is Satan with a vagina."

She giggles, biting on the tip of her index finger, and I can't help but admire her.

"I know. She's perfect."

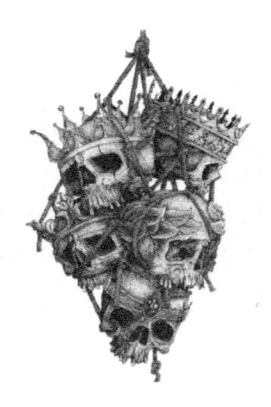

HE HANGS FROM THE ceiling, a hook shoved into his back, as Saxon and I take turns inflicting pain and torturing the truth out of him. He's loyal, I'll give him that, but I think that has more to do with the fear of what Dmitri would do to him than it does wanting to protect him.

Saxon stands across the room, throwing sharpened darts at him and cheering when one embeds itself in his dick. He groans in pain and a little vomit leaks from his mouth.

"Oh! I know!" she says suddenly. "Where's that bear trap?"

The Bratva picks his head up with newfound energy and his eyes widen. "B-bear trap?"

She bites her lip. "Think of a Prince Albert, just much larger. It's going to look so good on you."

As she turns around and goes to find a bear trap, he shouts. "Okay! Okay." He looks at me pleadingly. "Stop her and I'll tell you what you want to know."

"I *want* to know where Dmitri is," I tell him.

He pants heavily. "I don't know where he is."

Saxon springs up and goes to run out the door when he speaks again.

"But I know where he's going to be."

I glance back at Saxon and she winks at me, showing she plays the role of completely insane well. "That's even better."

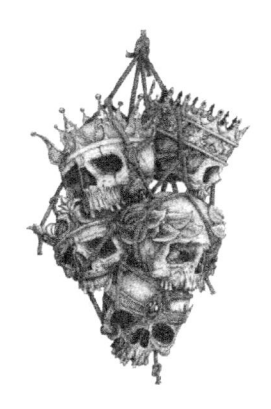

SAXON SITS IN THE hot tub with her head tipped back and her eyes closed, as if she wasn't just using someone as a human dartboard earlier. I stand beside Beni as he sprays the blood out of the shed. After all, if we leave it there, it'll start to smell.

"So, what's the game plan?" he asks.

"I'm not entirely sure yet," I answer him honestly. "He'll be at the Valenci Gala tonight, but so will plenty of his men.

I'd really rather not go in guns blazing and let innocent people get caught in the crossfire. There has to be another way."

Beni snorts. "Saxon is rubbing off on you."

"*Saxon* is a goddamn nightmare," I correct him. "Harley Quinn doesn't have shit on her. Hell, I think she even gives Viola a run for her money."

"You do realize the prom date she was talking about at Raff's funeral is the same one she castrated in the limo that same night, right?" He smirks, as if he's impressed by her antics.

I shrug. "He ditched her to have sex with someone else. I don't exactly disagree with her. He knew who he was dating. It's the other people she's killed that concern me."

Shutting off the hose, Beni closes the shed doors. "But that's what I'm saying. She *has* killed people. Saxon tortures comfortably but never delivers that final blow."

Looking over at her bobbing her head to the music that plays through the speakers, I smile. "She's saving her first kill for someone who truly deserves it."

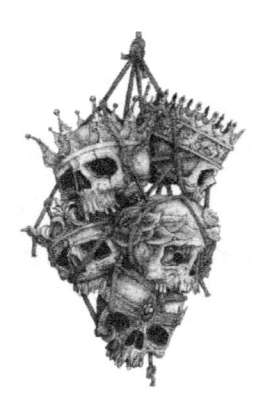

LOYALTY IS MORE IMPORTANT than most people give it credit for. And in my line of work, it's absolutely vital.

Which is why, as I stand in my living room surrounded by my most trusted men, I've never appreciated them more. They know what we're planning on walking into could end up getting them killed. And yet, they'll follow me straight into the fire anyway.

"Dmitri is an arrogant son of a bitch, but he's slick. He knows we're looking for him and has been staying out of view, but his image is important, which is why he won't miss the gala tonight."

Beni hands out a picture of him to Roman and Cesari. "To refresh your memory, this picture was taken two weeks ago, only hours after he killed Raff in cold blood."

"I'd rather there not be innocent casualties, but if it means getting him in our clutches, do whatever it takes."

The bedroom door opens, and all our heads turn as Saxon comes out with Viola. "We have a better idea."

She walks around the couch until she's standing beside me. Her hair is down and curled, which I'm guessing was Viola's doing. She's wearing a black dress that hugs her body in all the right places, but I could do without my men seeing the slit that goes almost all the way up the one side. But out of all of it, it's her shoes that catch my attention.

"Goddamn, Gabbana. How thin are those heels?"

Looking down at her feet, she lifts one leg to look at the heel and then smiles proudly. "I carved them into weapons."

"Focus, Kage," Viola says. "Your plan is great and all, but there's a chance Dmitri could get away in the chaos, and who knows when you'll find him again. Saxon and I have something else in mind."

If it were any other women, I'd tell them to leave this to the men. But maybe it's because I've seen firsthand what they both can do, or because telling them that would without a doubt make Saxon use her shank shoes on me, but I step back and gesture for her to go ahead.

"The floor is yours."

CHAPTER 17

KAGE

MENDING FENCES IS NOT SOMETHING THAT EXISTS much in my world. When someone gets themself on my bad side, it's final. The only exception I've ever made to that rule is with Raff, and that's only because I owe him my life. He could have let me go into the system. The Familia would have been his entirely, and I probably would have grown up addicted to drugs, taking out my trauma on people who deserve it much less than my current victims. But he didn't.

And that's why I owe him this much.

I raise my fist and knock on the door, hearing the sound of footsteps coming down the stairs. The door opens and Nico goes from annoyed to shocked when he sees me. I don't wait for him to greet me or ask if I can come in. I simply push the door open further and walk inside.

"Viola isn't here," he tells me.

"I know. She's at my house." *Coming up with ideas that are going to put me in an early grave if they don't go according to plan.*

"Oh." He turns and walks over to the couch. "Okay."

As I look around, I wonder how he and Viola are still

living here. I understand the whole *childhood home* sentimental value, but as I look at where Raff's recliner once sat, my stomach churns.

"He deserved so much better than what he got," I tell Nico.

He leans forward and rests his arms on his knees as he looks over at the same empty spot I am. "He really did."

I straighten my suit and turn to face him. "Losing a parent is one of the hardest things I've ever been through, and no matter how many times it happens, it never gets easier. But there is one thing that helps, and that's retribution."

Nico looks up at me. "I know, and I didn't mean what I said at the funeral. I don't think you're responsible for his death."

"I do," I say honestly. "Not entirely. If I had known it would end up with Raff getting killed, I would've gone after Dmitri first. But I do think it played a part, and that will stay with me for the rest of my life."

He shakes his head. "It shouldn't. You were avenging your father's death."

"Yes," I nod. "And now it's time to avenge yours. Dmitri is going to be at the Valenci Gala tonight. We're going to capture him, and we're going to kill him. I'm here to ask if you want in."

There aren't many times in my life I've seen Nico tear up. Mafia men don't show emotion because it makes us feel weak. But as he looks over again at where his father once sat, watching the football games every Sunday, his bottom lip starts to tremble.

"Abso-fucking-lutely."

DRIVING THROUGH THE CITY, dread settles in my stomach. There's no describing how risky this is, or how everything could go horribly wrong in an instant, but Viola had a point. If we're looking to catch Dmitri off guard, this is the only way to do it.

We get to the mansion shortly before the gala begins. Beni and I step out of the van first, with Nico and Roman following after. Saxon and Viola stand between the two in the back as we enter, making sure they're completely out of view. The only way this will work is if no one else knows they're here.

Making our way through the house, I find Mattia standing at the end of the hallway. He and Costello may have been useless when it came to finding Dmitri, but their connections to the Valentis proved valuable. He leads us straight to the security room, and the moment we enter, the two men in there get up and leave.

Beni sits down in front of the wall of screens and checks that all cameras are working while I wrap a protective arm around Saxon. When we agreed on this plan, after I gave the fight of my life against it, we did it knowing the risks. We're either coming out hand in hand, or not at all.

Her and I, we bleed together.

"You know what you're doing, don't you?" I ask Viola.

She fixes her black wig in the mirror and looks at me through the reflection. "Don't worry, Casanova. Let the women handle the dirty work."

Saxon chuckles and leans her head against my chest.

From the back, Saxon and Viola are identical. They're the same height with the same figures, and as long as Saxon's hair stays covering her back, you won't be able to see the top of her tattoo peeking out the top of her dress. It's a good plan; that much I can't deny. I just hope Dmitri is as unprepared as we need him to be.

I take a deep breath and let it out slowly.

Here goes nothing.

MY PALMS SWEAT AND MY heart pounds inside my chest as I watch the cameras. Seeing Dmitri socializing with others in the other room, acting like he hasn't a care in the world, it takes everything in me not to go in there and put a bullet straight through his temple. But that would be too easy. I want to take him alive, though I'll settle for him dead.

Roman is on the other side of the ballroom. He keeps a close eye on everything while staying inconspicuous. With so many different people roaming around, it would be almost impossible for Dmitri to pick him out.

"There she is," Beni points out as Saxon comes into frame. She keeps her head down as she makes her way over to the bar, picking up the drink Roman ordered for her. Even the chance of the bartender noticing her as she ordered was a risk we didn't want to take.

Picking his wives is something Dmitri takes pride in. He obsesses over them. Thinks of them as his property long before they actually belong to him. And Saxon was the first one taken away before he got the chance to destroy her, so it's no surprise when he notices the familiar, long black hair from across the room.

She keeps her back to him as Nico talks to her through the mouth piece, instructing her on what to do. Dmitri converses with a colleague, but we watch as he keeps glancing over at Saxon, trying to be discreet as he wonders who he is looking at.

After a moment, curiosity gets the better of him and he excuses himself. As he starts to cross the room, Nico speaks into the microphone.

"He's coming your way," he tells her. "Do it now."

I hold my breath as Saxon lifts her head and looks directly at him, letting Dmitri see that she's still alive after all. He stops in his tracks, his jaw clenched and angry. The flare of his nostrils gives away his rage, but he won't make a scene in the middle of everyone.

Saxon puts down her drink and gently pushes through the crowd of people as she heads down the hallway. Like we knew he would, Dmitri follows behind. I watch through the camera as Saxon turns the corner with Dmitri quickening his speed.

"Go now," I tell Viola.

She leaves the room and starts walking down the hallway in the same direction. Saxon turns into the security room and shuts the door just in time for Dmitri to turn the corner. I exhale, wrapping my arms around her tightly and kissing the top of her head. She watches the cameras closely, worried about Viola as Dmitri follows her, thinking she's Saxon.

Finally, Viola reaches the lounge and stands in front of the lit fireplace, her back to the doorway.

"Do we have an audio feed in there?" I ask Beni.

He presses a few keys and the sound kicks on just in time for Dmitri to come into the room. He looks Viola up and down, as if he can't believe she's standing there.

"You're supposed to be dead," he growls in his thick Russian accent.

Viola turns around and smirks, showing that she's not Saxon after all. "Sorry to disappoint."

She grabs the stun gun that was holstered to her leg and points it at him, but as she pulls the trigger, nothing happens. Her eyes widen as she does it again, only to get the same result.

It's malfunctioning.

Shit.

Dmitri laughs as he walks toward her. In one quick move, he grabs her and puts a gun to her head, using the girl as a shield as he stares into the camera.

"Give me Saxon or she fucking dies!" He screams.

"Viola!" Saxon shrieks as Nico and Beni run out the door.

She goes to follow, but I grab her wrist and pull her back, moving to stand in front of her.

"I have to help her!" she panics.

I shake my head. "You can't. That's exactly what he wants."

"But Viola!"

"Stay here," I tell her. "We'll get her. Just stay here."

Shutting the door behind me, I run down the hall after Nico and Beni. The three of us press our backs to the wall and keep our guns firmly in our grip. On the count of three, we rush into the room.

I've seen a lot of emotions on Viola over the years. She's always been one for the dramatics and a total firecracker. But as she stands there with Dmitri's arm around her chest and his gun pressed to her temple, I think this is the first time I've seen her scared.

"Get those fucking guns off me or I'll shoot!" he orders. "You know I will."

Nico looks at me pleadingly, and I nod. The three of us slowly put our guns on the floor, holding our hands up.

"I want Saxon," he tells me.

"Saxon is dead, Dmitri." I keep my tone grim to make it sound more believable. "You ordered the hit yourself."

"Fuck you," he sneers. "I saw her with my own eyes. Get me Saxon, or this one is coming with me." He grabs her chin with his free hand. "She's not as pretty, but I'm sure her mouth will feel good once I rip all her teeth out."

"You know I can't let you do that. Just give her back to us, and we can all go home."

He narrows his eyes on me. "You think I'm a fucking idiot? Give me Saxon, now!"

Pulling the gun away from Viola's temple, he fires a shot at Beni, striking him in the upper arm. My eyes widen as I watch him go down, groaning in pain. I swear, if this motherfucker takes the life of another person I care about...

"Saxon fucking Forbes!" he roars. "Now!"

Tears start to flow from Viola's eyes as she watches Beni. I can't tell if it's because she's in fear for herself or because she's worried about him. Beni looks up at her and nods, silently assuring her he'll be okay, but I don't have the time to unpack what that's about before Dmitri's temper goes up another notch.

"I'm going to count down from ten, and if you don't give

me Saxon by the time I hit zero, I'm going to empty this clip into all four of you."

His threat is a serious one, and as he starts to count, all I can do is hope that Saxon gets out of here safely. But as he reaches five, the voice of the one person I don't want to hear right now meets my ears.

"Don't hurt her," Saxon begs.

I whip my head around to see her coming into the room, putting herself directly in harm's way. Fear and horror take up my every emotion as I watch her get closer to him.

"You can have me," she tells him. "Just don't hurt her."

When Saxon is close enough, he throws Viola to the ground and grabs Saxon's wrist, pulling her against him. "Good girl."

He starts to pull her from the room, keeping his gun pointed at her head. But before he can make it out the door, Saxon closes her eyes. She pushes a pressure point on his arm that keeps him from pulling the trigger, while her foot rears back. The heel she so proudly carved into a weapon stabs him in the knee. While he's rendered temporarily defenseless, she spins around and grabs the gun, jamming the butt of it into his head.

Dmitri falls to the ground, out cold, as Saxon shakes off the feeling of his touch. The moment he's not a threat anymore, Viola rushes to Beni as Nico uses the zip ties in his pocket to tie up his arms and legs. I, however, walk directly into Saxon and wrap my arms around her.

"Go get Roman and tell him to bring Dmitri to the warehouse," I order Nico. "I need to get Beni to Antonio."

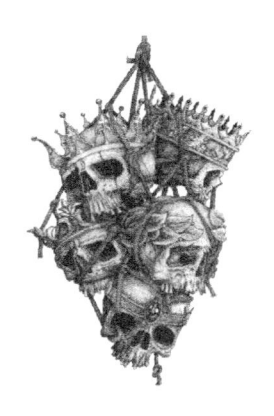

GUNSHOT WOUNDS, NO MATTER where they are, are never fun to deal with. They're painful, and messy, and the bullets can wreak havoc on your muscles. I watch in discomfort as Antonio works to take the metal out of Beni's arms. Viola stays faithfully by his side while Saxon comes over to me.

"What's going on there?" she murmurs.

I chuckle. "Your guess is as good as mine."

Beni glances over at me and rolls his eyes as he groans in pain. "What are you doing? Don't you have a scumbag to torture? Get out of here!"

Antonio pulls the forceps out, bringing a small distorted bullet along with it. Beni sighs in relief as he sees the worst of the pain is over now, but he still needs to be stitched up.

"He going to be okay, Doc?" I question.

He looks at Beni and nods. "It didn't hit any major arteries. He'll have some tenderness for a while and his arm might be weak until he rebuilds the muscle, but he'll be just fine."

"Ooh. I'll be a better shot than you," Saxon teases.

Beni scoffs playfully. "In your dreams, Kamikaze. Now, seriously, get out of here."

I nod. Now that I know he's going to be all right, I can

focus on making Dmitri pay for what he's done. Draping my arm around Saxon and heading for the door, I realize we're missing someone.

"Vi?" I say, getting her attention. "You coming?"

She looks down at Beni who nods. "Go. I'll see you after."

I glance at Saxon, seeing her just as confused as I am as Viola squeezes Beni's hand and then lets go. She walks toward us and when she notices the look Saxon is giving her, she smiles guiltily.

"What?"

Saxon snickers. "Nothing. Nothing at all."

THE FOUR OF US stand in front of the door, hearing Dmitri yelling from inside. Saxon and Viola look like they've waited their whole lives for this, ready to torture and brutalize until there's no part of him left the way God intended. I turn to face Nico and put out my fist.

"For Raff," I tell him.

He smirks and fist-bumps me. "For Armani."

Pushing the door open, we walk in, and Dmitri's eyes lock with mine. Seeing him chained to a chair and defenseless does unspeakable things to me. He glares at me with such disdain, but when I step to the side and he sees Saxon, it turns to straight disgust.

"Your father was right to want you dead," he sneers. "Such a waste of a pussy."

She giggles like the little psychopath she is. "Says the guy who wanted my pussy so bad that when he didn't get it, he threw a temper tantrum."

I slip the EpiPen from my pocket and walk over to Dmitri, jabbing it into his leg and dosing him with epinephrine. "I wouldn't want you to pass out during all the fun."

It's a trick I learned from Saxon, who really has been putting her pre-med major to good use. A dose of epinephrine will keep someone from passing out when the pain becomes too much, which is perfect, because I want him to feel every last second of what we do to him.

Nico holds the two large branding irons I had made for this very occasion, while Viola lights them with a blow torch. Once they're both a glowing red, he brings them over to me.

"Usually I'd save this for the end," I tell him. "At least that's what I did with Evgeny and Vlad, but I want you to feel it. The burn of their initials will linger in the background while everything else we do to you makes you pray for death."

At the same time, Nico and I push them against his chest, burning the initials A.M. and R.M. into his flesh. He grits his teeth to not give us the benefit of hearing him scream. Little does he know, that's the least painful of the things we have planned for him.

"Fuck you, you fucking guinea," he screams at me.

I chuckle as I toss the branding iron onto the ground. After today, I won't have a use for it.

My need for revenge against those who stole from me dies with him.

Grabbing a tube that is big enough to fit a baseball through it, with a funnel at one end, and a bucket, Nico makes his way toward Dmitri. The smell that comes from it has me turning and burying my nose in Saxon's hair. She giggles softly at me.

"Such a pussy," she whispers.

"Open your mouth," Nico orders.

Dmitri spits at him, droplets of saliva landing on his shoe. "You're just as weak as your father was."

I watch as Nico nods slowly and then puts his hand out. Viola hands him a metal contraption, and Nico puts it over his head. The metal slices his lip as it forces its way into his mouth and pries it open. Once he has access, Nico shoves the tube into his mouth and halfway down his throat. He takes an actual ladle from the bucket and starts to pour the liquid into the funnel.

"What the fuck is that?" I ask, cringing from the smell.

He shrugs. "Piss, shit, cigarette butts? I had Roman get it from a construction site port-a-potty."

The urge to gag is intense as I watch the mess go down the tube and into Dmitri's throat, despite his thrashing around. "Ro needs a promotion."

When he thinks he's had enough, Nico rips the tube from his mouth and pulls the device off his head. Dmitri immediately starts to heave, vomiting up some of the contents Nico just forced into his stomach. A mix of shit and stomach bile spews from his mouth.

"Enjoy that taste in your mouth," Nico sneers.

Dmitri tries to shout insults back at him, but his words get cut off every few seconds as he gags some more.

Saxon and I are next. I grab the sharpest pair of tree trimmers while she takes the heated iron. She steps up in front of him and he glares at her.

"It's a shame you're such a whore," he croaks. "I would've had fun knocking you around."

She doesn't answer. Instead, she smirks as she grabs his hand and holds up his pinky. Dmitri roars as one by one, we cut each of his fingers off, using the iron to cauterize the wound. About halfway through, Saxon winces and turns her head away.

"Going soft on me, Gabbana?" I ask as I cut off his index finger and she presses the iron to the opening left behind.

She keeps her head as far away from Dmitri as possible. "No. His breath just fucking reeks. Nico, you couldn't have saved that shit for last?"

"Right before he dies and doesn't have to taste it?" he argues. "What fun would that be?"

"Fair point," Saxon agrees.

Once all his fingers are gone, we step back and admire the stubs he now has for hands. The places where his fingers once were are black, burnt from the iron, and the smell of burning skin adds to the stench of shit and vomit.

Viola stands with her finger to her lips, observing him. "Get him up. I need him hanging."

With a glance at Nico, the two of us work together. We unchain him just long enough to tie his arms behind his back. Standing him up, we lead him over to the hook that hangs down from the ceiling. Saxon presses the button that lifts him into the air, dislocating his arms from the angle.

Having him where she wants him, Viola wheels over a meat grinder on a small table. The top of it is sawed off, making it so you can see the feed screw rotate as she turns it on. Saxon grabs a cattle prod off the table and follows her. Dmitri's eyes widen as he looks down at the meat grinder.

"The fuck are you going to do with that?"

"I'm making your dinner, silly," she tells him with sweetness in her tone. "You have to eat."

Viola undoes his belt and slides his pants and boxers to his ankles. His dick hangs in the open, and Viola shares a look with Saxon. Dmitri smirks proudly.

"That could've been yours," he tells Sax.

She rolls her eyes and looks away with a sound of disgust,

letting her wrist fall limp as she shocks him with the cattle prod to the balls. The electric shock causes a rush of blood flow to the area and his dick hardens involuntarily. He watches in horror as Viola raises the table up and even Nico and I have to turn around as his most valued appendage gets caught in the feed screw.

The scream Dmitri lets out rivals all others before them as his dick is ground up, with pieces coming through the cutting plate and landing on the table. Once he's completely castrated, Viola turns back to Nico.

"Brother," she calls. "I need you."

He throws his head back as he groans. "Why me?"

Saxon and Nico switch places, and as she passes by him, she presses the button and pretends like she's going to shock him with it. Nico jumps out of the way, and she giggles.

Dmitri's head hangs low, his eyes closed and mouth open as he tries to recover from the immense pain. Viola takes advantage of the moment, using tongs to pick up some of his ground dick and filling his mouth with it. He immediately tries to spit it out, but she holds his jaw shut.

"Hold him like this," she tells Nico.

He gags but does what she says as she takes a strand of leather and a 12 gauge needle, sewing his lips shut all the way across. Tears flow down Dmitri's face as he strains against them, but there's no use.

He's powerless.

Saxon takes my hand and pulls me toward Dmitri as Viola finishes. She grabs two knives off the table and hands me one. Then, she cuts two lines vertical and two horizontal into his abdomen, making a tic-tac-toe board. I roll my eyes playfully.

"You and your games."

The two of us play for the right to cut out his eyeballs. She wins the first one, cheering as I lift her up so she can claim her prize. The second, however, goes to me, but I choose to let him keep it. I want him to *see* my next move.

Staring Dmitri in the face, I flick my lighter open and shut repeatedly. He looks defeated, but it's not over yet. Nico grabs the can of gasoline and douses his legs with it. With a single bounce of my brows, I toss the lighter and watch as he goes up in flames.

His screams are muffled due to his lips being sewn shut, but his pain is evident as he thrashes around. After a few seconds, when the fire starts to spread to areas that could be fatal, I nod toward Nico and he puts him out with an extinguisher.

Dmitri breathes heavily through his nose as I step closer and grab his face, forcing him to look at me through the only eye he has left.

"I'm glad he fucked your wife," I sneer. "I bet she sucked his dick like a goddamn champion."

That angers him, making his whole body shake with rage. But it's quickly wiped from his mind as Saxon hands me the bottle of ammonia and I pour it over his blistering, third-degree burns. The pain is unbearable as he comes close to the edge, but the epinephrine keeps him from going all the way out.

Nico and I repeat the process over and over, until finally, I pour the gasoline over his head and watch as his whole body goes up in flames. He screams so hard that he rips his lips open. Blood flows down his mouth as he feels every moment of the most excruciating pain I can deliver.

And when he finally stops moving, there isn't a single person in this room who feels bad for him.

THE CEMETERY IS QUIET, void of any curious onlookers. I walk across the grass with a bottle of Cognac in my hand and three shot glasses. The air is cold against my heated skin, but that could be due to the overdose of adrenaline I got from earlier.

Standing between the two graves, I look down at the names of men who made me who I am today. A sense of pride settles over me, and I can't help but feel like they're here with me.

I did it.

I avenged their deaths and made their enemies pay.

Pouring out three shots, I leave one on each of their graves and hold my own in the air.

"This is to you."

Chapter 18

Saxon

SOMETIMES, IT ISN'T ABOUT THE KILL. SURE, taking someone unworthy of life out of this world is great, but playing with your victims is where the thrill is. Ending their life is the easy part. It's making them regret they were ever born that I'm interested in.

Kage sits beside me in the limo, handing me the mask he had made. "Are you sure about this? It's risky."

"Are *you*?" I ask.

He chuckles and shakes his head. "Not even a little, but you've more than proven to me that you can handle your own. It's time I stop treating you like you're anything less than my equal."

Hearing that come from his mouth is everything. I came into this world a prisoner and a pawn, someone who was taken for someone else's gain. A girl stumbling through her own life, not knowing what her purpose was until she was forced to face it head on.

And I came out a warrior.

I wrap my hand around the back of Kage's neck and pull him in for a kiss. "I love you."

"I love *you*," he replies. "Let's go make it so he can't sleep tonight."

An involuntary giggle bubbles out of me. "I think messing with him is my favorite hobby."

Over the last few weeks, I've taken pride in taunting and tormenting my father. The death of Dmitri Petrov was everywhere after he mysteriously vanished from a prestigious gala. If my dad didn't think we were coming for him after that, he definitely does now.

I started small, having a package delivered that was full of dead rose petals and a picture of the two of us. It was enough to make him look over his shoulder, but still could have been justified as someone obsessed with him or my death.

After that, I used a personal touch. He came out of work one day to find his car saturated, both inside and out, with antifreeze—the same thing he used to poison my grandfather. Taped to the steering wheel was a note.

Do they know what you did?

Because I do.

Tick tock, Tick tock.

That had him hiring extra security.

My favorite thing, however, was when I lit his office on fire. The one place that makes him feel most like a man of the elite. I waited until the middle of the night, of course. I didn't want anyone to get hurt that didn't deserve it. But imagining the look on his face as he sorted through the soot and ash was more than worth the lecture that I got from Kage about risking my safety.

Note to self: next time use a bazooka.

The point of tonight is to keep him on his toes. A masquerade ball is the perfect way to let him see me without actually *letting him see me*. Just seeing a woman with Kage will be enough to make the gears in his mind turn. And I can't wait to watch it drive him insane.

I look in the mirror, making sure that my brown wig is in place, and Kage helps me put the mask on.

It's beautiful, with black feathers and lace edges. It'll only cover the top half of my face, but that's all we need. Just enough to keep him curious but not enough to give it away.

"Ready?"

I nod, watching as Kage opens the door and climbs out. He turns around and extends his hand for me to take. Beni waits for us with Viola, who looks stunning as ever as she hangs on his arm. We still haven't figured out what's going on between those two, but whatever it is, they're both staying tight-lipped about it.

"Mr. Malvagio," a photographer calls. "Who is your date?"

I make sure not to look his way as Viola answers for me. "It's my cousin, Alexi. Isn't she gorgeous?'

"Could you have picked something that sounded any more like a stripper name?" I murmur lowly.

She grins deviously, letting me know it's payback for what happened in Rhode Island. "You asked for it, *Viola*."

"You both are! Mind if I get a picture?"

Kage shakes his head and holds his hand out, as if he's willing him to keep his camera down. "No pictures tonight, thank you."

I keep my head down until we get inside, but when we do, I can't help but admire how incredible this is. Coming to these kinds of events is one of my least favorite memories from my childhood. And growing up with rich parents meant there were a lot of them. But being here with Kage, and being old enough to drink, I don't entirely mind it.

"For a bunch of people whose whole life is crime, you sure do like to throw your money around at big parties," I tease.

Viola chuckles. "It's how they make up for what's in their pants."

I spin in Kage's arms and place my hands on his chest. "If I get you drunk enough, am I going to see what's in *your* pants?"

He puts a hand on my lower back and pulls me closer. "All you have to do is ask, baby. No alcohol required."

Viola looks over at us and rolls her eyes. "As adorable as you two lovebirds are, if you don't tone it down on the PDA, Dalton will figure out your secret in five seconds flat. He's dumb, not blind."

She has a point, so Kage and I put some distance between us, but that doesn't stop me from making a dig at her anyway. Besides, she earned it by giving me a name like *Alexi*.

"Oh, Ellis," I tease. "Always the sensible one."

Beni's brows furrow as he looks between the two of us. "Who the fuck is Ellis?"

"Is that the bar?" Viola asks, changing the subject. "Great. I'm parched."

IT'S HALFWAY THROUGH THE night and I'm starting to think my father isn't going to show, when I spot him in the corner of the room. He's talking to a few other men in expensive-looking suits, no doubt telling lies that make him seem like a decent person. The one thing that seems to be missing from his arm, however, is my mother.

I subtly glance around to see if there's any sign of her, but there isn't. Though that's probably for the best. If anyone would be able to spot me through a disguise, it's her.

Kage spins me carefully around the dance floor, but every time he pulls me close, he whispers another insult about someone in my ear.

"Do you see the guy in the blue suit to your left?" he murmurs.

I find who he's talking about and smile. "Yes?"

"He smells like cat piss."

My lips press together to keep me from laughing. "He does not."

Kage chuckles. "Swear to God. I had to sit in a meeting with him once and it took everything I had not to throw a bucket of soapy water on him."

This goes on all night. On the dance floor. At the bar. Sitting at the table. I've come to the conclusion that the only people here he can actually stand are the ones he came with, and even Viola depends on the day.

The feeling of eyes burning into the side of my head doesn't go unnoticed, but I know better than to make eye contact with him. It would give me away. So instead, I keep my attention on Kage and enjoy a night of quasi-normalcy with him. And when the night ends and I lie in bed, I bask in the knowledge that my father is probably lying awake and wondering who the woman with Kage was tonight.

But he'll never guess what I have planned for him.

CHAPTER 19

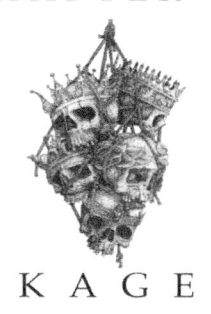

KAGE

Being feared by my enemies is how I like things. I never want them to know my next move, or trust that they're safe. I want them to know without a shadow of a doubt that if they cross me, there will be consequences, and that we will see them through. But at the same time, I'm not interested in an ongoing war that makes me spend all my time planning my next move.

Which is what brings me here.

I walk into Mari Vanna with Beni on one side of me and Roman on the other. Bratva members snarl at us as we walk by, wanting to attack but also not willing to risk dying today. We ignore them all and head straight to the back where the new leader of the Bratva sits. Erik is a younger man, around mid-forties, who most likely couldn't point Russia out on a map, let alone ever been there. But that's what happens when the three men who have ruled for decades all die within the same few months.

As everyone turns to glare at us, Erik's gaze lands on mine. He waves us over with two fingers and I take a seat on the chair opposite from his, while Beni and Ro stand on either side of me.

"You have a lot of balls showing your face in here after what you did to Dmitri."

I chuckle and rest my ankle on my knee. "Why? 'Cause

from where I sit it looks like what I did helped you step into the power seat. Or do you *not* have control of your men?"

He hums with a smile and waves for his men to carry on —a silent signal that everything is fine and to mind their own business. "Is there something you wanted, or did you just come to question my authority?"

"I just wanted to make something clear, so you know it came straight from my mouth," I tell him. "If any of your men try to come after me, in retaliation for the men I've killed or otherwise, I will not apologize for the bodies that end up at your doorstep, even if it declares war."

Erik opens his mouth to talk, but I hold one finger up to signify that I'm not finished yet.

"But, I believe this city is big enough for two organizations, and as long as you stay on your side of things and don't overstep into my territory, I will not be wasting my time with the insignificant."

He rubs his hand over his bare chin, as if there's supposed to be hair there. "So what? Is this you wanting some kind of truce?"

I chuckle, shaking my head. "No. I don't make deals with scum, but the vendetta I had against your former bosses was a personal one and doesn't pertain to you. Keep it that way."

With that, I get up from my seat and hold my head high as we leave, knowing the message was properly relayed. What they do with it is on them.

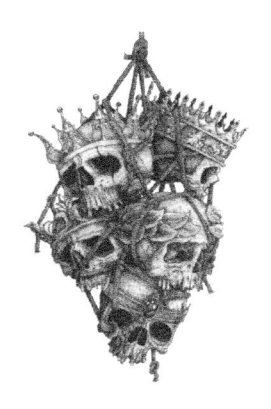

I SIT AT THE small table in the corner of L'Artusi as I wait for my guest to arrive. By my third glass of water, I almost think she isn't coming, when the door opens. Scarlett has Kylie's hand grasped firmly in hers as I stand. She looks around the room, exhaling when she sees me.

"Thank you for meeting me," I tell her as she reaches my table.

Her hair is thrown into a messy bun, and she looks like she's had one hell of a day, but she gives me her best smile. "Of course. I'm sorry I had to bring my daughter. She woke up sick and I had to keep her home from school."

"It's no problem at all."

She pulls an iPad out of her purse for Kylie to play with as I order the little girl a ginger ale for her stomach. Once Saxon's sister is settled, Scarlett turns her complete attention to me.

"So, what is this about?" she asks. "You said that Raff left a message for me with you?"

I nod and pick my phone up off the table. "Before he died, he recorded this for you just in case we needed it. In the event he wouldn't be here to explain it himself."

Scarlett takes my phone and hits play, her eyes instantly tearing up as Raff's charming face comes on the screen.

"Hey, Scar," he says. "I wish I could have been there to explain this to you in person, but if you're watching this, it seems I'm unable to do that. Please remember the strong woman your father raised you to be as you listen to this message. It'll help get you through everything you're about to hear."

She swats a tear from her cheek as she listens carefully.

"Your husband is not the man he makes himself out to be. Deep down, you've always known it. Silas kept him in line for the most part, but when Dalton's hunger for power got stronger, he turned on him. Kage is going to show you a lot of evidence showing the role your husband played in Silas's death, as well as Saxon's. I need you to trust him enough to listen, because your safety and Kylie's future depends on it.

"I've always loved you like a daughter, and even though I'm not there to help you through this, I promise you it's all going to be okay."

The video ends, and I can't tell whether she's more upset or confused, though it's probably an equal mix of both.

"Raff was such a good friend of my Dad's," she explains. "If it weren't for him, I don't know how I would have gotten through the loss. Did you know him well?"

I nod respectively. "He was my father, for all intents and purposes, since I was ten years old."

She gives me a tearful smile. "Then you must be a good man, too."

Kylie pushes the headphones off her ear and pouts at her mother. "Mom, I feel icky."

"Actually, I have a message for you too, little one," I tell her, getting up and squatting down in front of her. She gives me her full attention as I boop her on the nose. "Your sister loved you *very* much."

Her eyes light up. "You knew my sister?"

"I did, and she used to talk about you for hours. Said you were her favorite person ever."

A grin spreads across her face, like having that title is the greatest accomplishment she's ever made in her short little life. She puts her headphones back on and engrosses herself in the video she's watching while I sit back down.

"I had no idea you knew my daughter," Scarlett says.

I smile the same way I always do when I think about Saxon. "I more than knew her, actually. I was married to her."

"Excuse me?"

Reaching into the folder, I pull out our marriage certificate and a picture of us from the ceremony. We're standing in the middle of my office, with Saxon in a white gown my stylist picked out for her. She's smiling brightly as she stares up at me.

Scarlett looks at the photo and covers her mouth with her free hand. "She was always so beautiful."

"That she was," I agree. "It was a small ceremony. She was planning on coming to tell you and introduce me to you, but Dalton never gave her the chance."

It doesn't matter that we got married only hours before the meeting with Dalton, or that originally it was meant to be an insurance plan, because there's no going back from here. She and I are in this for the long term. If she wants a divorce, she'll have to *actually* shoot me this time.

Putting the picture back on the table, she presses two fingers to her temple. "I don't understand. Why would Dalton do something to harm Saxon? He loved his daughter."

"What do you know about Dmitri Petrov?" I ask her.

She purses her lips. "Not much. Just that Dalton used to have business meetings often with him."

I breathe in and let it out slowly. "Dmitri was the leader of the Russian mafia. When your father passed away and Dalton was going to inherit all of his properties, he reached out to Dmitri and struck a deal. He would give everything to him, plus your Saxon's hand in marriage, in exchange for power."

"H-he would do that to our daughter?"

"He did a lot more than that," I say softly. "When Saxon found out, she came to stay with me. She was never at Duke University or any of the lies he told you. She was in the Hamptons with me, where Dalton couldn't force her to be with Dmitri. But when he learned she was pregnant, she was no longer of use to Dmitri. Your husband was furious, and he had her killed for it."

Lying doesn't usually bother me, but in this situation, I wish things could be different. This is a woman who loved her daughter so much that the pain of losing her is all over her face. But as I think back to the conversation I had with Saxon this morning, I know I have to respect her wishes.

Saxon lies with her head on my chest as I run my fingers through her hair. For a moment, I think she fell asleep, but then she picks her head up and looks at me.

"What time are you meeting my mom today?" she questions.

I check the time. "In a few hours."

She nods and puts her head back down, but I can almost feel the pain radiating off of her.

"We can put it off, you know," I suggest. "Get your revenge first and fill Scarlett in after. She and Kylie can know that you're alive. You can still have them."

Sitting up, she takes a deep breath and sighs. "No. I can't. The mafia life is no place for either of them, but it's exactly where I need to be. It's better for them if they believe I'm dead."

I want to argue her reasoning. To try to explain that we can find a way to keep them in the dark, but I don't know if that's true. And when she gets up and walks away, I know her decision is final.

. . .

"I was going to be a grandmother?" Scarlett cries. "But she was so young."

"It wasn't intentional, I promise. But we were excited all the same."

She looks down at her lap and smiles. "God, I miss her."

I give her a minute to compose herself while I pull another folder out of my briefcase. When she's ready, I slide it over to her and keep my hand on top, knowing the contents aren't something you can dive into without caution.

"I need you to brace yourself. The information I'm going to share with you will be shocking and it will hurt, but someone once showed me that the best decisions are made when you're faced with all the facts."

She nods and after taking a deep breath, she opens the folder.

We sit for hours in the little Italian restaurant, and I comfort her the same way Raff would as she learns about everything.

Her husband's involvement in her father's death.

Evidence of the role he played in Saxon's death.

Her father's involvement in the Familia.

Her husband's affair.

Each thing is no easier to hear than the last, but I can see where Saxon gets her strength from. She holds it all together, and when she walks out with her head held high, I can see why Saxon misses her so much. Maybe if my mother had that fire, she would still be alive.

Chapter 20

Saxon

MY GRANDFATHER ONCE TOLD ME REVENGE IS worth nothing, and that the best way to get back at those who have wronged me is to kill them with kindness. But while I love him dearly, he's the same man who told me to keep my hands to myself, and that's not nearly as much fun.

A nostalgic feeling creeps up the back of my neck as I walk through my family's new house. It's a cute place, way larger than they need, on the outskirts of the city. Even though I never lived here, it holds my mother's warmth. It's one of the things I missed the most.

Pictures of me hang on the walls, something that would have haunted my father if he had a conscience. On a table off to the side in the living room is a picture of my mom and me. It was when we went on vacation to the Bahamas. I'm sixteen, with sun-kissed skin, smiling happily. Next to it is a vase of flowers. They look fresh, and it wouldn't surprise me if Mom keeps up on switching them out—keeping my memory alive.

As I walk up the stairs, the butterflies on the door give

away which room is Kylie's. The walls are painted pink with gymnast silhouette decals and her medals on display. Everything in here smells like her, and there's a pang in my chest at the thought that I'll never see her again. But it's for the best.

Heading back down the stairs, I go into the kitchen to grab the sharpest knife I can find. One thing our chef has always been big on is knives. I just never thought it would be of such use to me until now.

Once I have what I need, I make my way toward my father's office. It's located directly to the left of the front door, right past the stairs, with big glass panel doors. Everything about it looks identical to the one he had in the penthouse, the only difference being the location of the safe.

Pictures of all his accomplishments hang on the wall, as if he's become something to be proud of. What a joke. I wonder what all these people would think about him if they knew the truth. If they *knew* that he tried to give his daughter to the leader of the Russian mafia in exchange for power, and when that didn't work, he tried to have her killed.

But they'll know plenty about him after today.

I sit down at the computer and use everything Beni taught me to hack into the security cameras. I remove what was captured of me entering and walking around the house and loop it over, making it look like the house has remained empty. With my help, Beni hacks in from a hotel a few blocks away so he can take care of the rest.

The only thing left to do now is wait.

ONE THING ABOUT MY father is that he's always had a passion for the fastest and most luxurious cars. He thinks that the things you own are what make you as a person, and if you're not arriving in style, you're bound to fail. So it's no surprise that I can hear him drive all the way down the street and pull into the driveway.

He whistles as he walks up the front steps, unlocking the front door and coming inside. But when he steps in his office and sees me sitting in his chair, his face pales. I cross one leg over the other and smirk.

"What's wrong, *daddy*? You look like you've seen a ghost."

His mouth opens and closes repeatedly before he can form a single word. "Impossible."

"Why's that?" I tease. "Because you had me killed?"

"We buried you," he says.

I smile as I inspect my nails. The black manicure Viola did earlier couldn't have come out better. "Yeah. Funny thing about closed caskets though. You never *really* know what's in them, or *who* is in them, for that matter."

He takes a step back, scrambling to pull his phone out of his pocket, but he doesn't get far with it. I pull out a gun with a silencer and fire it once, shattering the screen and effectively rendering it useless. His eyes widen as he stares back at me.

"You don't want to do that," I tell him, scrunching my nose.

"What the hell happened to you?" he sneers. "This isn't the daughter I raised."

I chuckle as I stand up. "You're right. I'm *definitely* not her, because you succeeded in killing me. The old Saxon is dead. Like *dead* dead. But that's okay. Really. I should thank you, because this new one? She's much more fun."

"Don't act like I'm the only traitor in this room. You willingly went back to him. I couldn't let my grandchild be born a Malvagio."

Hearing him refer to my baby, the one he ripped from my womb before he even had a chance to live, strikes a nerve. The darkness settles in as I want nothing more than to slit his throat, but I'll settle for a stab to the stomach.

My plan depends on it.

I reach behind my back and grab the knife I took from the kitchen. Before he even realizes what's happening, I shove it into him, right beneath his rib cage. The blade slides through him with ease, and I don't think I'll ever tire of that feeling.

"Saxon," he croaks as I pull it out.

His blood covers the knife, turning it a metallic shade of red. "What's wrong? You think you're the only one capable of killing your family?"

Holding his stomach, he falls to the floor, while I stand above him and watch. His hands are covered in blood as it oozes from the wound and he sprawls on his back. It wasn't a fatal wound, not immediately anyway, but it still hurts like a bitch.

"You know, I considered letting you live," I tell him, "for Kylie's sake. But then I realized killing you would be doing her a favor. It's better for her if you're not around to use her. To abandon her when she needs you the most. To offer her to someone without her consent in exchange for money and power."

I get down on my knees beside him and run my free hand over his face as he watches me in fear.

"If you're thinking they're going to save you, they're not. Mom and Kylie should be long gone by now, with all the proof of your little affair and enough money to last them the rest of their lives. And you? The only place you're going is to hell."

Bending down until my lips are by his ear, I whisper softly.

"This is for me."

I raise the knife up above my head and plunge it into his rib cage, repeating the motion over and over. Blood splatters everywhere, splashing onto my face, making it hard to see. And when I'm done, and he lies there, lifeless, all I can do is smile.

Wiping my face with my shirt, I get up and go to sit in the chair.

Down falls the king. Now we just wait for his queen.

RIGHT ON SCHEDULE, THE door opens and heels click against the door as she comes in. I sit on the chair in the corner, keeping me out of sight. She checks the living room first, then the kitchen.

"Dalton?" she calls.

Even the sound of her voice hits me where it hurts. There

was a time when that voice brought me comfort and solace. When I would listen to it give me advice and promise me that everything was going to be okay. But those days are long gone, never to return, because she killed me. I may not be dead, but she left damage that will stay long after my scars fade.

The sound of her heels comes closer until she's right outside the office. A frightened gasp echoes through the foyer and she screams.

"Dalton!"

I watch from my seat as Nessa runs into the room, dropping to her knees and trying to wake my father despite his blood-soaked clothes. She's too engrossed in her own panic to realize I'm here. Laying her head on my father's chest, she sobs over the loss of a man who doesn't deserve to be mourned.

"Daughter of New York's Elite Dies Tragically at twenty-one," I say, reading the headline and alerting her to my presence.

Nessa picks her head up, spinning around to see me across the room. "Saxon?"

She fakes a smile and jumps to her feet, but as she rushes to hug me, she's met with the same knife plunged into her stomach. She inhales quickly and grips the knife, effectively putting her fingerprints all over it. Kage would say it's risky, letting her have a weapon, but there's no doubt in my mind I could take her if she tries anything.

"I have to say, the picture that goes with the article is grade-A acting," I tell her as she pulls out the knife and lets it fall to the floor. "Truly. You deserve an Academy Award for that performance."

Squatting in front of her, I tilt my head as I watch her panic internally. Her hands are covered in blood, both hers and my fathers, as she stares at me in disbelief. I don't blame her. She was always the tough one, while I would rather curl up in bed with a good book.

I guess shit changes when your best friend tries to kill you.

Her purse lies on the floor, the contents spilling from inside after she dropped it trying to make it to my dad. I pick up her phone and shove it in front of her face to unlock it. After it lets me in, I dial 911 and wait for them to answer before I play the recording Beni created.

"911, what's your emergency?"

"I need the police. I killed my boyfriend and I tried to kill myself, but I don't want to die. I just wanted him to leave his wife."

Nessa watches in horror as her voice plays through the speaker, saying things she's never said. I watch her closely, waiting to hit the mute button if she tries to scream, but deep down, she's a smart girl.

She knows I'll kill her if she tries.

The 911 operator types vigorously in the background. "Okay, just stay calm. Is he breathing?"

I press the appropriate recording. "No, he's dead. I'm so sorry. I didn't mean it."

"It's okay. We all make mistakes," the dispatcher says. "What's the address where you're at?"

Grabbing my phone from where I left it on the desk, I put it to her head and hold the phone in front of her. She leans her head against the bookcase and breaths heavily as she recites the address. When she's done, I run the barrel down the side of her face, mouthing *"Good Girl."*

"Okay. I have officers on the way. Can you stay on the line with me?"

I hang up and toss the phone beside her.

"Why?" she croaks.

A dry laugh bubbles out of me. "Next time you try to kill someone, don't wear the designer heels they bought you for your birthday while doing it. Though I have to say, faking my mom's tattoo and trying to frame her for it was clever. You really lived up to your name...*Monster*."

She coughs and then whimpers from the pain. "So kill me then. If I'm such a horrible person, fucking kill me."

I shake my head slowly, smirking at her. "No, death is way too easy for someone like you. I'd rather see you rot behind bars, getting beaten to a pulp every time I feel like offering a person on the inside some money. And then, when I think you've finally suffered enough, I'm going to rip you out of there and kill you myself."

"I'll tell them." Her voice is weak but it's there. "I'll tell them everything."

"Aw, babe." I smile sweetly at her. "I'm dead, remember? Thanks for that solid alibi."

Sirens sound in the distance as the door opens and Viola looks at me impatiently. "Sax, come on. We have to go."

She comes into the room, dodging the blood that stains the carpet and grabs my wrist. Nessa's brow furrows as she looks at her.

"Who are you?"

Viola grins and flips her hair. "I'm you, with better fashion tastes and life choices."

I grab my things, including my father's cracked phone and the bullet that shattered it, and head for the door. But just before I leave, Nessa's voice rings out.

"You're going to burn in hell for this."

I stop, looking back at her and lifting a shoulder in a careless shrug. "I'm not worried. The devil and I get along just fine."

KAGE

I used to think that feelings were fire. They ripped through your body and made you weak, ripping you apart from the inside out. I spent most of my life blocking them out, only to have them rush back in at the sight of an eighteen-year-old society princess with an attitude that stopped me in my tracks.

Over the time we've spent together, I've never felt so much pain. The devastation I've had to face has threatened to send me over the edge. But at the same time, it's also brought me her. Someone who didn't try to save the beast because she was becoming one herself. My perfect match, my other half.

My favorite little psycho.

Her heels click against the tile floor as she makes her way through the house, dressed in all black and looking like sex and candy. Her eyes meet mine and she smiles, licking and nibbling at her bottom lip as she imagines all the things she wants to do with me. To me. *For me.*

Saxon Malvagio is something fucking else.

Wild.

Dangerous.

Sinful.

And mine.

EPILOGUE

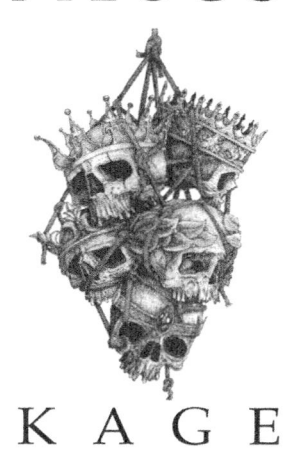

KAGE

FIVE YEARS LATER

There's something calming about the ocean. The sound it makes as it crashes against the shore, rushing up the sand, just to be pulled back in. I sit on the back deck and watch as Saxon plays with our son at the water's edge. They run around, splashing each other and having the time of their lives. And I don't think my heart has ever felt so full.

I have to admit, when Saxon mentioned wanting to move out to the little town we found in Rhode Island, I wasn't immediately on board. My whole life was in the city. My business. The Familia. I had responsibilities and people counting on me.

It wasn't until Khaos was born that my view changed.

Six pounds, five ounces. He was everything I never realized I needed. With Saxon's black hair and her piercing blue eyes, the only things that boy got from me are my temper and the love I have for his mother. And as he started to grow up around the same life that has brought so much loss, I knew a change was necessary.

I didn't have to give up everything. I'm still the don of the Cosa Nostra with Beni as my underboss. I just choose to run things from here while Roman rules New York City with the same merciless fist as I did as my Capo de Capi—with Nico and Cesari faithfully at his side.

Thanks to Scarlett keeping her word and signing the properties over to me, there's still a city to run. She and Kylie moved to a small town in the Outer Banks where Kylie is working tirelessly on achieving her dream of the competing in the Olympics. Pictures of the inside of their home show they still keep pictures of Saxon, frozen in time but still very much loved.

The only big sacrifice I had to make was my company. It was the only thing I built from the ground up, the one part of my life that I did by myself, without the help of anyone else. While Elison was more than happy to take it over, and I knew I was leaving it in good hands, it was difficult to part with.

But it was more than worth it.

Saxon looks over at me, and her eyes lock with mine. A broad grin stretches across her face, looking happier than ever. And as she turns her attention back to our son, I can't help but feel the same.

ONE THING THEY DON'T tell you about before you have kids is their attitude. At four years old, Khaos has gone through the baby stage, the terrible twos, and the threenager stage, and it feels like every year he gets bigger, so does his ability to verbally bitch-slap me.

Someone should have warned me that Saxon was going to give birth to a tiny dictator with a selfishness that rivals my own.

"Okay, little man," I tell him as I finish putting on his favorite Batman pajamas. "Let's see what we can do with that wild hair of yours."

I run my fingers through it and let the moisture hold it in place. Usually, I'd just ruffle it around. He's going to bed soon, anyway. But tonight, I decide on something different.

Using both my hands, I style it into a fauxhawk and chuckle at the result.

"There, now you look like a little badass."

His eyes widen and I know I've fucked up when he gets up and jumps around his room. "Badass, badass, badass."

I pinch the bridge of my nose. "Khaos, what did I tell you about repeating Daddy?"

He stops and covers his mouth as he giggles.

Saxon comes in moments later, looking like an irresistible temptress. She's wearing a red dress that Viola bought her last Christmas and a pair of black boots. Her tattoo peeks out the back of the dress and reminds me about everything she's been through and how hard she fought to survive.

Goddamn, I'm a lucky man.

"Mommy!" Khaos shouts.

She keeps her legs pressed together and squats down so she's at his level. "Look at you! Your hair looks so cute!"

"Daddy said I look like a badass!"

Snitch.

Saxon's brows raise as she glances over at me. "Did he now?"

"I think you should just accept the fact that our son is going to have a very diverse vocabulary," I tell her.

"Mm-hm." She stands up and takes Khaos's hand. "Come on, handsome. Auntie Vi is waiting for you downstairs."

He squeals excitedly. "I love Auntie Vi!"

The three of us head downstairs where Viola is standing in the living room. The second Khaos sees Viola, he lets go of Saxon's hand and runs full force toward her.

"Auntie Vi!" he screams.

She bends down so he can run straight into her arms. "Semen Demon!"

I snort while Saxon turns around and buries her face in my chest to hide her laughter.

"You can't keep calling him that," she tells Viola.

Viola cocks a brow at her. "Why not? It's his nickname!"

Instead of fighting with her, Saxon rolls her eyes and walks over to our son. She runs her hand over his cheek and kisses his forehead.

"You be good for Auntie Vi, okay?" Then she turns her attention to Viola. "And no horror movies this time."

Viola bounces Khaos on her hip. "How else is he going to live up to his parents?"

"No, Viola," Saxon tells her.

She groans but agrees. "Lame."

With my hand on Saxon's lower back, we head out for a date night that we don't get nearly often enough.

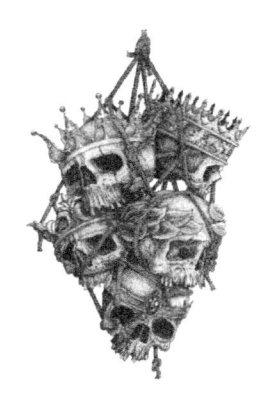

WHEN WE FIRST CAME to this strip, during the impromptu road trip to make Saxon feel human again, I never thought that it would eventually be my home, but I don't mind it. It has a cozy kind of feel to it that I never had while growing up in New York.

The two of us walk hand in hand, just enjoying the cool summer air after a few drinks. It's a little busier than it is in the off season. While this town isn't exactly a tourist attraction, some people still manage to find it. But Saxon rests her head against my arm and hums happily anyway.

Or at least until she jolts forward and spins around on her heels.

"Hey, pretty thing," a drunken man slurs. "How much?"

"Excuse me?" we both say in unison.

He looks up at me and his nostrils flare as he focuses on Saxon. "I'm sure your sugar daddy pays you well for your time, but I just want one night. How much?"

Before Saxon can answer, I move her so she's behind me

and place myself in between them. "My *wife* is not for hire, so I suggest you make yourself scarce before I show you what happens to a man who touches a woman that isn't his."

Too drunk to realize the severity of my threat, he rolls his eyes and turns around, stumbling away like my words held no weight. Once he's a safe distance away, I pull Saxon close and put my hands on her ass—covering his touch with my own.

"Are you okay?" I ask her.

She chuckles. "Yes, caveman."

I bend down and press my lips to hers, only for her to pull away after a few seconds.

"Do you ever miss it?" she questions. "The adrenaline of it all? The thrill?"

It's a valid question. While I've had to get my hands dirty every now and then, I've taken more of a back seat since achieving my revenge. But there's always a little bit of an itch inside of me that craves it.

My gaze locks with hers, and I admire the fire that still burns inside of her. There's a vicious glint in her eyes that relays the message loud and clear.

Gabbana wants to play.

"Get off of me!" shrieks a woman only about fifty feet away.

But he doesn't listen. He pushes her into the garbage can and tries to force her dress up on the middle of the sidewalk.

"Stop! Someone help me!"

My decision is made for me.

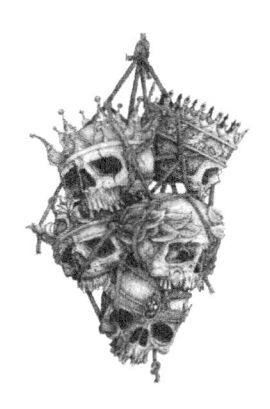

THE BASEMENT IS DARK, with a winding hallway that hides the room we're in from anyone who may venture down here by accident. The drunken rapist hangs from the ceiling with his arms above his head, thrashing around as he pleads for us to let him go.

"I'm really sorry," he cries. "Please. Don't do this. I'm a good man."

Torture tools of all shapes and sizes are scattered across the table, waiting to be used and made bloody. Our victim glances over at it and sees his fate right in front of his eyes. His begging stops as he realizes there is nothing he can do.

Saxon and I turn to face each other, and she smirks as we move at once.

Rock.
Paper.
Scissors.
Shoot.

Curious about Knox and Delaney?
Check out their story here.

Want more Kage and Saxon?
Check out their wedding scene.

Still not enough?
Check out this bonus chapter.

ACKNOWLEDGMENTS

Okay, so real talk for a second.

Writing most of this duet was hard. I'm not even going to sugar coat it or pretend it wasn't. These characters and their story had so much detail and emotion that went into it. Listening to them and feeling them show me everything, it was overwhelming. I don't think I've ever doubted myself or my writing so much in all the time I've been doing this. I didn't believe I could deliver what you deserved. I didn't think I was capable of writing something so dark and so full of pain, and yet so beautiful at the same time.

I was able to push through with the help of an incredible team promising me I was on the right track. And with my husband, my family, and my friends making sure that I took a break when my anxiety got a little too difficult to handle. And with the patience of my editor and proofreader who are goddesses when it comes to dealing with me and helping make my books perfect.

But the main thing that kept me going were my readers. You believe in me even when I don't believe in myself all that much, and I'm not sure you know what that means to me. Or how many times I've been in the middle of a horrible feeling of imposter syndrome when one of you will say something about one of my characters or email me something you loved in a book of mine.

Long story short, from a girl sitting at her computer, tearing up from the love I have for all of you, Thank You. My life is forever changed by you and I am forever grateful.

If you enjoyed this book,
please consider leaving a review.

**xoxo,
Kels**

ABOUT THE AUTHOR

Kelsey Clayton is a USA Today Bestselling Author of Contemporary Romance novels. She lives in a small town in Delaware with her husband, two kids, and dog.

She is an avid reader of fall hard romance. She believes that books are the best escape you can find, and that if you feel a range of emotions while reading her stories - she succeeded. She loves writing and is only getting started on this life long journey.

Kelsey likes to keep things in her life simple. Her ideal night is one with sweatpants, a fluffy blanket, cheese fries, and wine. She holds her friends and family close to her heart and would do just about anything to make them happy.

KELSEY CLAYTON

Malvagio Mafia Duet

Suffer in Silence

Screams in Symphony

North Haven University

Corrupt My Mind *(Zayn and Amelia)*

Change My Game *(Jace and Paige)*

Wreck My Plans *(Carter and Tye)*

Waste My Time *(Easton and Kennedy)*

Haven Grace Prep

The Sinner *(Savannah & Grayson)*

The Saint *(Delaney & Knox)*

The Rebel *(Tessa & Asher)*

The Enemy *(Lennon & Cade)*

The Sleepless November Saga

Sleepless November

Endless December

Seamless Forever

Awakened in September

Standalones

Returning to Rockport

Hendrix *(Colby and Saige)*